I0654985

EVERYONE HAS A TESTIMONY; NO ONE FALLS FROM HEAVEN!

This book is a result of the author's imagination. It is fiction. However, many of us have testimonies like this one, but we are ashamed to tell them. To be ashamed of your testimony is to be ashamed of the work Jesus did for you on the cross.

You can read my testimony in *A Diversified Black Woman: I Feel So Blessed* (Volume One) and *A Diversified Black Woman: I Was...I Am The Face* (Volume Two).

"Everyone has a Testimony. No one falls from heaven. Most people dedicate their lives to God through processes. Sometimes it doesn't happen overnight and very rarely does it happen instantly."

"It's not about how many books sold. For me, it is about not sitting on my gifts and dreams."

"Life is too great to live like it is too short."

SHAYTALES PRESENTS

EVERYONE HAS A TESTIMONY

WHY YOU MAKE MY BROWN EYES BLUE

(A Novel)

VOLUME ONE

ShayTales

www.shaytales.com
Email us: rw4rp@shaytales.com

Cover photography, cover concept, and book design by Shay 7

Cover design by Keith Saunders for MarionDesigns.com

Library of Congress Control Number: 2012931146
ISBN 13: 978-0-9850589-0-6
ISBN 10: 0985058900

ADULT CHRISTIAN FICTION

"You can twiddle your fingers and wait for someone to discover your talent or you can use every dime you have to discover yourself. Sometimes you have to achieve for others to believe."

ACKNOWLEDGMENTS

I would love to acknowledge the **Davis family**, my paternal family. Forgive my failing to acknowledge you all in the first book. I love you all very much.

DEDICATION

This book is dedicated to God, Jesus, Holy Spirit, me, my mother, my boys, my family, my friends, my supporters, and people who pray for me and desire to see me happy in every area of my life.

In memory of

Annell Davis (paternal grandmother) 1916-2012
My grandmother Emma (Mama) 2003
My aunt Yvonne 2001
My father Donald (Honkey) 1999
My aunt Trina 1996
My cousin James (Pnut) 1994
My cousin Bianca (BB) 1993

CONTENTS

Introduction 3

1 Tick-tock biological clock 5

2 Time to meet the family 72

3 It was Malissa 98

4 He left me 110

5 Trying to go on 135

6 The woman who got bit by a snake 147

7 Here comes the bride 155

8 Mrs. Underwood 166

9 The big 40 175

10 Trouble brewing on the schoolyard 191

11 Two by Two they went 197

12 The battle is not yours, it's the Lord's 210

INTRODUCTION

"God takes a life of drama and makes it a Masterpiece."

Everyone has a testimony. As much as we like to pretend, no one falls from heaven. Although some highfaluting Christians walk around like they have always been saved, most Christians have experiences that they are not proud to share. But no matter how ugly your experiences are, you have to share them in order to bring others into the faith and to give those in the faith confidence in God. When a testimony is sugarcoated it loses its value. It loses its healing power. As a writer, I take pride in being Christian; however, I also take pride in writing "realwords4realpeople."

God is the cornerstone of every story I write because only God can take a life of drama and make it a Masterpiece. Only God sees the beauty in us that many people fail to see. Hence, *Everyone Has a Testimony* will always be about people who walk through the valley of the shadow of death but fear no evil because they know God is with them. If they do not know it from the outset, they learn it during a course of events.

MY PRAYER

My prayer is that these books will remind you of your
own trials and triumphs
They will be a source of inspiration to those that need it
They will be a source of wisdom to those that heed it
They will give strength to the weak
And be a source of confirmation to the meek
For God is always working in our lives
God is always by our sides
And oftentimes, God is carrying us
Because we all experience things that leave us having
no clue
Of what to do
We all have testimonies
And they must be shared
To help others realize that God is there
And though it hurts sometimes, God cares

CHAPTER ONE

TICK-TOCK BIOLOGICAL CLOCK

I awoke this morning staring at the ceiling as I clung to my bed. I said to myself, "Girl, it's hard being you." Breath tart as I yawned. It's time to get up and get my day started. No sex last night but plenty of conversation. I didn't see anyone I wanted to go home with. Every guy that I talked to had too many problems, and I didn't want to get involved with more drama. I have enough drama of my own. What I desired for one night would have meant more to them.

It's hard being single, and I never claimed it was easy or stress-free. It's not the life I choose, but it seems to be the life for me.

I'm a 37-year-old first grade teacher who is free for the summer. I have no kids, never been married, and never had a proposal. I don't know why. I'm gorgeous—let the truth be known. I'm a five-five bombshell if I must say so myself. I take pride in keeping myself in shape and looking good. I don't have anything else to do. I'm single

5

and always ready to mingle. I am a teacher in the day and a party animal at night. I don't allow my partying to get in the way of my work, and I don't allow my work to get in the way of my partying.

However, one time my career and partying collided. I dated this guy who I later found out was the father of one of my students. He lied to me about being single. He lived with my student and my student's mother who was his longtime girlfriend. His girlfriend was huge with a constant scowl on her face. I didn't want any problems with her. I broke it off immediately without exposing him, and he didn't expose me. However, it didn't end there. I often had meetings with him and his girlfriend in reference to their daughter who wasn't doing so well in class. Oh how I prayed that my student would do better with her academics. I even paid extra attention to her to get her on level. She didn't get any better, so I was obligated to meet with her parents often. I had to sit around a man that I had copulated with and pretend as if I didn't know him in front of his longtime girlfriend. It was scary. I kept thinking I was going to mess up and call him by his nickname, which would have suggested familiarity. Once that school year was over, I was elated.

The longest relationship I've had lasted two years. We didn't make it because I didn't want us to make it. I couldn't see him fathering my kids. He is very unattractive physically. Maybe I am a shallow person, but I couldn't imagine my kids looking like him. Perhaps I will seem better if I tell you that although we no longer date each other romantically, we are the best of friends. His name is Mike.

During our relationship we got along well, we had great sex, and he was mentally and physically good to me. But Mike was just one of my victims — someone to kill time. I fell in love with his beautiful heart and how he loved me unconditionally. My mother says I'm too picky, and sometimes I think she's right. But I will know Mr. Right when he comes, and he will know me. Until that time comes I want to do what I want to do, go to every club in Hot-Lanta that I want to go to, and spoil myself with as many relationships as I can maintain. If my mother had her way about it, I would be in church every Sunday with a dress on to cover my knees.

I set out to do something different this summer. Last summer I taught summer school, but this summer I decided to chill-out. I want to feel myself, go places, and meet people. I bought myself a hot brand new car, a 1997 Gold Maxima with tan colored leather interior. Just thinking about my baby made me walk over to my bedroom window to look down at her. I wanted to make sure she was doing okay.

My neighbor's husband stood outside washing their cars. We share a huge two-level duplex. They are pretty good people, but sometimes the husband is a little flirty. His body is nice, and he knows it. He is chiseled to perfection. I have never seen a man with so many muscles and rips percolating and palpitating all over his body. He looked like a man in a weightlifting magazine. He is not too big—just right. He knows he is attractive, and whenever he washed their cars he would let everyone else know too. He didn't wear a shirt or shoes. He wears these very short blue jean shorts with shingles at the bottom. What man wears shingles cut into his shorts? I couldn't understand that, and I couldn't understand why Stacy allowed him to cut shingles in his shorts. If I had a husband, he could never walk around with shingles at the bottom of his blue jean booty-shorts. He couldn't walk around with booty-shorts on!

Cameron's body glistened as the sun shined down on it. He is a flirter for sure—a chick magnet. Yet, his wife is no mouse of a woman. She has him on a very tight leash. She controls his every move. Stacy is older than he is, six years. Besides her husband washing his car in the nude nearly, Cameron and Stacy are very good neighbors to have.

"Hi, Cameron." I spoke to him first because he spotted me in my window.

He smiled from ear to ear. "Hi, Demisha!" He had a toothpaste smile—the kind where you saw the sparkle. He heard and saw everything in the neighborhood, and he smiled at everyone. It is as if he has an automatic smile button located somewhere on his body. I think that is why he made me sick at times. He smiled without a reason to smile. I always suspected him of something. I shouldn't say that about him because he has only been nice to me. But he seems like the type of man that would try to sleep with you if you wanted to sleep with him. Nothing overtly he has done—just covert behind that big beautiful smile.

I pushed my window down and walked into the bathroom to take a quick shower to start my day off. I felt pretty good. It was beautiful outside.

****

I looked clean as I rode down the street in my new car thinking of what I was going to get into for the day. I made my first stop my mother's house. I always had to see her. It seemed to start my days off right after I looked into her beautiful face. My mother didn't live too far from me. She resided about ten minutes away. Being the only child, my mother and I liked living close to each other. My mother didn't drive, so I had my space when I needed it. She rode the bus a lot from place to place whenever I couldn't transport her.

She is a 57-year-old retired nurse—Christian. After her retirement, she decided to work three days out of the week at a nursing home. She's such a great nurse that the nursing home allows her to choose any three days of the week to work.

My mother is my mentor. She put herself through nursing school, raised me alone, bought herself a home, and put me through college. I never really knew my father. He past when I was 2 years old with an unusual heart disease. My mother and father were only married three years when my father past away. My mother keeps lots of pictures. I have my father's beautiful smile and straight teeth. He was quite handsome. My mother said I am the spirit and image of my father.

My mother must have heard my car pull up. As I entered her driveway I saw her peek out of the window. I opened her front door with my key. "Mama, your baby is here. What did you cook, Mama?" She walked up to me, and I wrapped my arms around her and gave her a big juicy kiss on her lips.

"Nothing, baby. I thought you were coming to take me to dinner."

I let her go and walked toward the kitchen as she followed. "No, Mama. We just had dinner together two days ago. I will take you out Tuesday. Tonight I have to party, honey. You know your baby." I took a seat at the kitchen table, grabbing a piece of fruit from the center.

"Where were ya last night? Ya partied last night." She said with the dishcloth in her hand and her hand on her hips.

"Mama, that was Friday, and this is Saturday another one of my partying days. I am not some little kid, mama. So get up off of my lifestyle, please. You know how I am. I have been this way for years now." I propped my leg on the seat of one of the other chairs.

"Yes and don't ya think it's time for ya to settle down? God doesn't like ya partying and hip-hopping all over the place ya know. Ya act like ya eighteen. Ya not a kid anymore."

"Of course I want to settle down, but I can't settle down if a man is not in my life to settle down with. And you don't know Mama, I might be hip-hoppin' for God." I giggled. I knew that was going to burn her up. Mama didn't play about God. You can talk about anyone but her God.

Her eyebrows lifted and shifted. "Listen here! I don't care how old ya are, missy. Don't play with God! Ya don't need a man to come in ya life for ya to settle down with God. God can deal with ya better when ya by ya-self anyway. God will send ya the man. But first ya got to get right with God. Ya have to get in position." Mama was serious.

"Mama, I am not playing with God. God knows my heart, and he knows you want grandkids. If he doesn't know, I know. I have heard this ever since I turned thirty." I rolled my eyes up in my head and took a bite of my fruit.

She moved around in the kitchen. "People always say God knows my heart. But what about ya spirit, soul, and ya body, child? He never sees ya body in church! And as for the grandkids, ya biological clock is ticking, baby. If it hasn't ticked out already!"

"Anna, please don't go there. You're starting to act like your sister Kissy May. You're on me about God. You're on me about settling down with a nice man. And you're on me about kids." Whenever my mother got on my nerves I would address her by her first name.

She stopped moving and turned to me. "Well, she is my sister. Ya know Barbara is pregnant? Kissy May is a grandmother three times already, and now Barbara is pregnant."

"Mama, Aunt Kissy May has three children to your one child, and Barbara is only 18 years old. Where is her husband? She has it backwards, doesn't she? As holy as Aunt Kissy May is, I know they are not celebrating about Barbara being pregnant without a husband. She shouldn't be having anyone's baby. She's still living at home with her mother, and she's never going to get a husband as long as Aunt Kissy May is in her business. That woman is nosy!" I tooted my nose up.

She giggled. "Yeah, she is, isn't she?" My mother and I both laughed as she took a seat at the table with me. Bringing up Aunt Kissy May changed the tone of the conversation.

"I am sorry, baby." She took a deep breath. "I

am not getting any younger, and neither are you. I want ya to get saved, live right, and get ya a good husband. That way ya won't have to be at them clubs so much. Ya looking for somethin' at them clubs, and what ya need aint there. And I want some grandkids so that I can spoil them like crazy before I leave to be with God." She said pinching my cheek.

I put my hand on hers. Then I spoke gently with a touch of humor. "Listen ol' lady." I laughed. Mama eyes got big and her mouth dropped. "Mama, you're not going anywhere. I am going to find a husband and have some kids. Well, my husband is going to find me."

"That's right. I know, I know. I need to chill. Right?" She leaned over and kissed me.

"That's right, chill-out. Everything is going to be all right, ol' lady. I promise you that one day I am going to be very holy. I will have a dress on to cover my feet. I'll have a big fat country God-fearing husband who can put down a pot of collard greens by himself. And I'll have so many kids that you will put me out of your house before we get in good." I joked.

"No, I won't either! Kids will bring some life to this place. I don't know about that collard-green-eating-husband because ya don't cook. And I know he doesn't expect me to cook 'em. Nah, we'll leave that collard-green- eating-husband where he at. Cooking for you is enough." She giggled.

I stood up. "Well, mama, I am going to get out of here. Lady's get in free tonight, and I must go get my boogie on." I took another piece of fruit.

She stood up too. "It's early right now." She wasn't happy to see me leave so soon.

"Mama, it takes preparation, baby." I danced around her playfully, grabbing her hand leading her to the front door. "No seriously, I just remembered Mike and I have a lunch date. I must keep this one. I forgot about the last one."

"Why are you and Mike not married? Ya see each other more than any regular friends I know." Mama didn't understand Mike and my friendship.

"All right Anna. What did I tell you about Mike? He is just not my type. I wouldn't want my kids to look like him. We both know that Mike is not the handsomest man in the world."

"But Dee, he is beautiful inside, and he just adores ya. God never picked his kings by their looks. In fact, David — "

I interrupted her. "Mama, please! And that beauty in the inside is the reason Mike is my friend on the outside. We don't have to go into the Bible, mama. I got to go, honey. I love you, I love you, I love you." I kissed her lips repeatedly, keeping her from talking as I opened the front door.

I walked to my car as she stood at the door waving and blowing kisses to me. My mother is truly my heart — one of the best people I know.

But she is on a level with God that is beyond me. And she worries about me because I am not there yet.

As I drove down the street I called Mike on my cellular phone to confirm our lunch date that I had suddenly remembered. "Hey, Mike. Boo, I didn't forget our lunch date. Did you forget?"

"No, I was waiting on ya to call me. I called ya house and left a message on ya machine. So I knew you were already on the prowl. Are we going to take my car or your new car? Ya know I wanna borrow it one day."

"We'll take mine, and maybe after it is a few days old we will trade cars for a day or two." I laughed.

"Okay, well com'on and get me. I'm waitin'."

"Where are we going? Did you find somewhere? I am tired of the same ol' food. I don't know what I have a taste for today."

"No, we'll jus' ride. You have a new car. I don't wanna go directly in and eat lunch anyway. I wanna see what ya new wheels are about." He giggled.

"I'm going out tonight. You wanna come?" I hoped he answered with a yes. Most times Mike was my partner in crime. It was rare that he turned me down.

"When do ya not go out? I might, we haven't

been out to a club together in two weeks. But me being busy haven't stopped you I'm sure."

"And you know it. I have to relax! It's summer, baby! The kids drive me crazy during the school year. I should be at your house in ten minutes. Hot alert! Hot brotha in the car next to me. He cannot stop looking over here."

"Will ya get over yourself? He is probably admiring ya car or the tires on it." Mike hated on me.

"I don't care how hot my car is, a man will never miss alllllll of this. You know what I'm working with. My tires are better than any car tires."

"Damn girl, you are a mess. Okay, see ya when ya get here." Mike hung up. My narcissism disturbed him at times.

Mike is a wonderful man. He is so sweet, and I enjoy being with him. He has such great energy. I cannot describe the chemistry we have, but he is such a pleasure to be around. I just don't want to marry him. I am very serious about how I want my kids to look. Mike is a very dark man. But his skin is one of his attractive physical qualities. His skin is beautiful and smooth. His teeth are perfect. I have never seen teeth so perfect in my life, and I have some beautiful teeth. However, he has a huge nose and small beady eyes. He is very unattractive physically to me. His features just don't fit or blend.

Although I think he is unattractive, Mike attracts lots of women. I think it's his charm. He also dresses and smells good. He has his own home, a $65,000 two-year-old sports car, and his life is together. The only thing that he is missing is his dream wife. And during our two-year love relationship he intimated many times that I was her.

I met Mike at a business function, and I knew right away that if he and I ever got involved, it wouldn't go far. Well, it went further than I ever expected. I didn't think it would last two years, but Mike is such a charming man that I got comfortable with him. After I broke up with him we remained good friends, and our friendship blossomed from that point on. A lot of people don't understand it. My mother being one of those people, but it doesn't matter as long as Mike and I understand it.

I called Mike on the phone as I pulled up in his driveway. "Mike, I am here. Come on out of the house."

He pulled back the curtain in his bedroom window and smiled as he held his phone. "Okay, I'll be out." He waved at me.

Mike walked out of his front door setting his house alarm system with his key fob. He was casually dressed, fly as usual. He always got an A+ from me when it came to his dress code. The brotha could dress — no matter the occasion. He had a way with colors and accessories. Mike owned more shoes than the average woman.

He walked around my car — checking it out. He smiled from ear to ear. It met his approval. He opened the passenger door. "Girl, this thing is nice! I didn't know ya went leather inside. Ya did it up, Baby-girl. This is bad! I am proud of ya!" He tinkered with the knobs on the console.

"Well, Mike, I had to do it right because you know how long I had my other car." I giggled.

"No, I don't know. How long did ya have ya other car?" He asked sarcastically.

"I had that car ten years, man! Ten years! I just tried to take care of it, so it was time for something new for me!"

"Really. Girl, ya should have had a new car a long time ago! I will never drive a car ten years! I don't care what kind of shape it's in. Who the hell does that? Only you — cheap!"

"Well, Mike, I got used to not having a car note, and now I have a new car with a fat car note!"

"What are ya paying, Baby-girl?"

"$350 a month!" I gasped. "And some change, man!"

"Girl, that is okay, especially since ya have it fully loaded. I just think you've been without a car note so long ya think ya should pay less than $300.

And that is never going to happen with leather seats, Baby-girl."

"I know, I know. I am happy with it. I just closed my eyes while I signed the contract. I convinced myself that I needed a new car. I hate being cheap about certain things."

"I know ya do. I'm glad you were not cheap this time. I love this car, and it rides so well. Pull over and let me drive it." He unstrapped his seatbelt before I could pull over.

"Okay." There was no traffic behind us, so I pulled over to the curb. Mike and I switched places.

Mike got his butt cozy in the driver's seat. He snapped his seatbelt in place, gripped the steering wheel, shifted the car in drive, and pulled off. "Baby-girl, I love this car! I love the way it drives! I might have to get me one of these or drive yours all the time!"

"No, you won't either! And have your women hunting my car down when they have caught your tail doing some mess! I think not!"

"What women? Please, I am only seeing two women, and they know the deal. They know I am not committed to either one of them — stop playing. If something happens to ya car while it is in my possession, I'll pay for it."

I was getting hungry and tired of us driving around. "Let's eat there, Mike!" I pointed at a restaurant. "We haven't tried that place yet."

"That place sells Philly steaks and fries. Is that what ya feel like eating? Ya know today is my day to pay. Are ya sure ya don't want something more expensive like ya usually do when ya know it's my turn to treat?"

"Mike, I can't believe you! That is terrible. I don't always pick expensive places to go when it's your turn. You have the choice when I treat, and I have never told you where to go. I always pick because you never know what you want." I hit his shoulder playfully.

"Well, I guess I have manners and ya don't. Hey, I love ya and it doesn't bother me. I have money. Ya just an underpaid teacher, so I expect a salad or sandwich and fries from ya." He teased. "I just ask can a brotha get a cola to drink sometimes instead of water."

I laughed. "Water good for ya! The doctors say it all the time."

"I know, but damnnn! A cola never hurt nobody!"

"You're right about me being underpaid. I need a raise right now. Come on clown lets go. I am hungry." Mike and I got out of the car. I grabbed his arm at his elbow, and we bounced into the restaurant.

We ordered a two-foot-long Philly cheesesteak, a huge basket of French fries, and a pitcher of lemonade. The restaurant was really nice. It was more like a sports bar, but there were a lot of families there. Mike and I talked as we usually did while we awaited our food.

"So why have ya been avoiding me?" Mike asked.

"Avoiding you? Mike, I only missed one of our lunch dates. I forgot to call you, Boo. Anyway, listen. I went to see my mother this morning before I came to get you, and she was killing me with this marriage thing. She wants some grandchildren. And she talks about how my time is running out — my biological clock is ticking. On top of that you know she wants me to get saved and live for the Looord. I am really getting tired of hearing it." I rolled my eyes up in my head.

"Well, it is Demisha. I mean, ya know I am ya boy. Therefore, ya know I am only gonna tell ya the truth, not what ya wanna hear. Ya mother was probably being nice when she said ya runnin' out of time. To be honest, I think ya ticker has ticked out! Ya eggs are probably dried up." He smirked.

"Mike, it's disrespectful to talk about a woman's eggs. You went further than my mother, dude. It's not like I am not trying. I haven't met a good man." I leaned my head on my fists as my elbows rested on the table.

"Ya a wonderful woman. That's why I love ya and would rather be ya friend than nothing at all. But babbbbyy, ya selfish and too stuck on ya-self.

Ya too fickle about everything, and sometimes ya have to compromise."

The waitress brought the food over and placed it on the table. "God this food looks good!" I sat up straight.

"I hope ya not too hungry because I might overdo it today." Mike cut the sandwich. The sandwich was smoking, and looking at the cheese stretch made my mouth salivate.

"Well, we might need to order another sandwich later because I didn't have breakfast. Some of Mama's fruit."

"All these fries they gave us, we'll be all right. As I was saying, ya have to stop wanting someone so perfect and everything ya way." Mike passed me a cut of the sandwich.

"Mike, I think you and my mother need to leave me alone. Y'all act as if I should just settle for any ol' body, and I don't feel how you guys feel. I must admit that I have had my share of men, but good men I don't think so." I took a bite of my sandwich.

"What about me? I'm a good man." He looked up at me as he tossed his sandwich around in his mouth. "This thing is hot!"

"You didn't see the smoke while you were cutting it? You need to slow down. It's not going anywhere. Look at me, take-smaller-biiiites." I facetiously said.

"I saw it, but I can handle the heat. I like big bites. I have to taste my food. I can't taste it taking lil bites like you. It's good too — some kind of special sauce they have on it. I wonder what it is." He continued tossing the food around in his mouth.

"Yeah, your shirt probably likes it too. You have some on it."

"Damn, I hate that." He looked at the sauce on his shirt and continued eating.

"Here, get the sauce off your shirt, please. Mike, you really are hungry." I handed him a napkin.

"It's really good."

"Back to what you said. Yes, you are a good man, and I must say a brotha has his thang tight too. But Mike you are not the man for me."

"Okay, clean that up before I say something because that didn't sound too good."

"Hell, you talking about my eggs didn't sound so good either. My eggs are sensitive. They have feelings too. But you didn't let me finish, nut-head. We make better friends, and I don't want to lose that for anything in the world."

"Hell, I know how to be ya friend and ya man. It's not hard. Ya jus' didn't want me."

"Nah. You are too sweet for me, and you give

me everything I want. I need a man who is going to be mean sometimes, so I won't abuse him." I turned my head slightly away and popped fries in my mouth as I looked at him from my peripheral vision. I hoped the torrent had subsided.

It was silent for a moment. It took Mike a moment to break away from his love affair with his food. "Whatever. So I'm bad because I know how to treat someone I love? See, you women do a good brotha wrong." Mike shook his head from side to side and commenced to loving his food again.

"Oh, Mike, please. You know I love you. We will be old as dirt still keeping our lunch dates and taking our families places together. I can see your tail now. You will probably have about three more kids and a beautiful Spanish wife." I chuckled — anything to keep the mood flowing smoothly.

"Why does she have to be Spanish? I love me a sista and ya know that. Don't be giving me no Spanish woman, black as I am." He lifted his glass of lemonade to his mouth.

"I don't know why I said Spanish. I guess that is just the kind of woman I see you with — someone out of your race as my mother would say. You're so charming, Mike. You can pull any woman. Most Spanish women have some black in them anyway." I giggled.

"I know that, but I like me a sista! A full blooded sista! That is how I am and how I will be.

Sistas are beautiful and strong. I like a strong woman."

"I know you do. What strong man wouldn't? We have to come back to this place. Their food is great. You are really enjoying it. The meat is probably precooked, but everything else is so fresh."

****

Mike and I spent the rest of the day together, and later on that night we were off to the club. Whenever we went to the club together we sat at the same table, but we gave each other space so the other single people in the club could read that we were not a couple. Mike would often approach other women to dance. And while he was gone, a man would come over and ask me to dance. So it worked well. We never stopped each other's flow.

This particular night we had a table that faced the front door of the club, so we were able to see everyone as they walked into the club. There was this one guy that I couldn't seem to take my eyes off. He shined to me. He had on all white — very clean. My eyes followed him as he found himself a seat. He was very attractive, beautiful brown complexion and curly hair. He looked to be about six-feet tall. I liked them tall, but I normally attracted to a darker skin tone.

"I'll be back, Baby-girl. I'm going to ask this lady to dance." Mike stood to his feet.

"Okay." Good, I thought to myself. I can stare down the six-foot stallion I saw enter the club. Normally when a man would see me staring he would rush over to my table. I hoped this time wouldn't be any different, so I hypnotized the handsome specimen with my gaze. When he took notice of my gaze I gave him total eye contact without batting, and then I crossed my legs very sensually. After that, I knew he was coming over to my table. If he didn't, I would assume he was gay.

After I got his attention, I turned toward the dance floor and watched Mike and his partner dance. I had not turned away a minute before I felt a light tap on my shoulder. I turned my head around, and there stood the handsome specimen that I stared down. He was more gorgeous up close than he was far away.

"Did I scare you?" His deep voice took over my space.

"No." I liked what I saw. I couldn't keep my sexy squint going because his beauty made me open my eyes wide. I wanted to take it all in — inconspicuously check him from head to toe.

"May I have a seat at your table?" He asked.

"Why sure."

"That's not your man on the dance floor is it?"

"Oh, no! He's my best friend."

"Oh, I saw you watching him. I don't want to cause any trouble. What's your name?" He smiled.

"Demisha, and what's yours?" In my head I said, I don't care what your name is because you are fine! But I kept my cool. I didn't want him to know that I was impressed with his physical appearance.

"My name is Melvin, but all my friends call me Mel." He held out his hand.

I shook his hand. "I will call you Melvin for now because I'm not so sure I will be your friend later." We both laughed.

"You have a wonderful sense of humor and a beautiful smile too."

"Why thank you. Yours is not so bad either." I put my sexy smirk on — slight smile with pouty lips.

"I don't dance well fast in case you're wondering why I didn't ask you to dance."

"No, I wasn't wondering." I pushed my chair closer to his because the music drowned our conversation.

"Do you slow dance with strangers? Well, I'm not a stranger anymore. You know me now."

"I-don't-know-you." I chuckled. "But if you're asking whether I will slow dance with you, sure. I come to enjoy myself. I'm not stuck up."

"Do you get a lot of men asking you to dance while you're sitting next to your best friend?"

"No, not really but he goes and ask other ladies to dance. And when he does that, just like you did, men will come over to me. We give each other space so that people will know that we are not lovers, just friends."

"You're a beautiful young woman. You have the sexiest legs I have ever seen." He paused as if he was thinking about what he had said. "I hope it was okay for me to say that."

"Thank you. It's okay with me. If you like it, say it."

"So do you come here all the time?" He looked into my eyes as he awaited my answer. He hoped I wouldn't answer immediately because he didn't want to stop making love to me with his eyes.

I blinked and shifted my head. I didn't like him searching my soul. I wasn't going to give him anything he hadn't garnered. "No. I get out to different places because I love to party, and I don't have any kids."

"I hear you. I love to party too, and I come here at least once a week. I'm not a party animal. But I don't have a woman or kids, so I do this to get out of my house. I love being around people. I love this club out of all the ones I have been to because the crowd here is slower." He pushed his chair even closer to me.

"Please. What club is slow? You mean this club has a more mature crowd?"

He leaned into my ear to make sure I heard him. I could tell he desired to be closer to me too. The chemistry was there. "Yes, that's what I mean. I am 35 years old. An old man like me needs a slower pace. A young woman like you can handle the faster crowd."

I raised my head and leaned over toward his ear as he held his head closer to me. "A young woman like me is older than an old man like you. I am 37 years old and proud of it."

He raised his head up and looked at me in disbelief. "You're older than me. I don't believe you! And here I thought I was hitting on a younger woman." He laughed.

"Well, I can't do anything about what you believe." I blushed.

"You look just as good as some of these women who are claiming 25 years old." I knew he wasn't gaming me. He was really shocked by my age.

"Well, I should. I don't have a husband or any kids."

"You're right about that because those are two things that can age you I heard." He chuckled.

"I don't really see it like that. I said I don't have a husband or kids to say that all I have is time to devote to myself. So I should look good for my age and someone else's age too."

"Yeah, I hear you. They are playing a slow song now. May I have this dance?" Confidence sprouted him to his feet. He held out his hand.

"Why yes." I stood up and eagerly placed my hand in his hand. He led me to the dance floor. This man was gorgeous—not a flaw in sight. And I looked for one. Even his breath made me feel like I was in a flower garden where bees trampled the petals because of the sweet aroma. The breath was always important to me. You could be handsome on the outside, but if you opened your mouth and it reminded me of a dumpster, there was no need for us to continue our conversation.

I have actually had to hurt a few men because of their deadly breath. Bad breath and smelly feet were deal breakers for me. I couldn't even have a one night stand with a man with smelly feet or atrocious breath. It just made my stomach turn something awful.

Melvin was a wonderful slow dancer. His feet glided across the dance floor as he held me close. On some of the fast songs we remained on the dance floor and continued to dance slowly. We danced the night away. At the end of the night Melvin and I exchanged phone numbers.

Mike drove us home from the club in my car.

"You and that guy danced all night." Mike commented as he drove.

I was leaned back in my seat, but I perked up to talk about Melvin. "Yeah we did, didn't we? I really like him. He is very attractive and a marvelous conversationalist."

"Well, I'm happy that you're happy. Sometimes you can be so hard to please you know, and that makes me afraid for you." He said seriously.

"I don't try to be, Mike. I think it's just the way I am." I squirmed in the seat trying to get comfortable.

"It is. And that's why most of the time I am afraid for ya. I don't want ya to be alone. I love ya for who ya are regardless of how ya are. I want ya to be happy. Everyone deserves to be happy." He laid his hand on mine.

I lifted my head up. "I know you love me, Mike. That's why you are my best friend. I know your love is real. I trust you with my life." I rested my head back and closed my eyes.

I awoke from Mike shaking my shoulder. "Baby-girl, we are here. Ya too tired to drive home, so come on in and take one of the other bedrooms."

"Yeah, you're right." I raised my head up. Mike got out of the car, and then he walked over to the passenger side and helped me out of the car.

I stood to my feet and wrapped my arm around his waist as he held on to me.

"I don't know why I am so tired. It came down all of a sudden."

"Ya danced all night, and ya had a great time. That's how ya so tired. Not to mention how we have been out all day and night long. Let me unlock this door." He released me for a moment.

Once we got inside Mike led me upstairs to his guest bedroom where I had stayed many nights not because of fatigue more of intoxication. He took off my shoes and helped me put on one of his big shirts to sleep in. Mike tucked me in and kissed my forehead. "Thank you, Mike. I'm exhausted, Boo." I turned over on my stomach and held my pillow tight.

"I know ya are. I know." He cut the light off and walked out of the room. I never had to worry about him trying to sleep with me or getting uncouth with me. He gave our friendship so much respect.

That next morning I got up following the intoxicating smells of food in the air. I loved Mike's cooking. This was what I liked most about staying over Mike's house. He would always get up and cook such a big breakfast. He could cook his black butt off! A connoisseur of great food, he never disappointed me.

I was so hungry that I stumbled as I walked

downstairs. "Are you okay?" He heard the clunk.

"Yes, I'm fine. I smell that food. I smell it! I smell it! What do we have, Boo? Whatcha cookin'? What do we have, Boo? Whatcha cookin'?" I asked melodiously.

"We got pancakes with blueberries." He followed my lead. He jumped up and down pointing at the food as he called it out.

"Mmmm. Yeah, yeah!" I danced.

"We got cheese and eggs." Mike twirled around.

"Mmmmm, come on! Come on!" I danced around.

"We got bacon, fried cris-ppppy." He rapped and danced.

I started beat-boxing with my mouth and tapping on the counter. "Yeah baby! Dat's what's up! Anything else! Dat's what's up! Anything elllllse! Anything elllllssse! Dat's what's up!" I made scratching sounds as if I was a Deejay on an LP.

"We got sausages and biscuits. Ssssausages and biscuits. Ssssausages and biscuits. Ssssau-sssau! Ik, ik, iiikkk uh! Sssau-sau! Ik, ik, iiikkk uh!" Mike rapped and scratched his imaginary LP.

"Talk to me, talk to me! We got it going on!" I

gave Mike a high-five. We laughed. We were always teasing and acting like kids when we were alone.

"I knew ya were going to be hungry. I started to stay in bed and make ya mad."

"Yes, I would have been highly upset. You are so stupid. I come downstairs acting crazy, and you just follow right along. I know we have been around each other too long." I giggled. "I'm ready. Let me go wash my face and my hands! I'm starving worst than Marvin." I ran toward the stairs like a kid.

Mike laughed. "Girl, you are silly! All a man has to do is cook for ya, and he's gotcha!"

Mike and I sat at his kitchen table eating breakfast. "This is why I like to stay over your house! Your butt can cook." I raised a forkful of pancakes to my mouth. "You the only black person I know that have fresh blueberries in the morning." I shook my head from side to side.

"Whoever ya marry better cook good or they will be in the poorhouse! If ya don't do nothin' else, you gon eat. I don't understand how ya eat so much and stay so fit. It befuddles me."

I stopped chewing the food in my mouth for a moment. "Nah, you didn't say it befuddles you, did ya!" I giggled. I made fun of Mike using the word befuddle. He spoke so much slang at times that befuddle sounded strange coming from him.

"It is what it is. I can eat until the cows come home!" I continued eating then I lifted my head and stop chewing for a moment. "The cows can come home, and I'm still going to eat. My metabolism is good, baby. Me and food like this!" I crossed my fingers and held them up.

"So ya really liked that guy last night, huh?"

"Yes, I really did even if I must say so myself. It was that conspicuous?"

"Ya danced with 'em all night! You and I would usually dance the last dance of the night, but ya had a ball with ol' dude." Mike had a slight grin on his face.

"You didn't do so bad yourself. I saw you and ol' girl talking together all night. What's with her?"

"She was nice, but she has four kids. What the hell am I gonna do with four kids! I can't deal with four kids."

I laughed so hard I almost choked. I had to drink something. "Boy, four kids will be good for you." I teased.

"We exchanged numbers, but nothing serious will come out of it. I have one of my own, and all-ah her kids under ten years old!" Mike continued eating and shook his head from side to side in disappointment.

"Oh, I know you wouldn't go there. With all

of her kids under ten, one of her men are still somewhere around the corner. I don't think I would have told a man that my first night meeting him." I shook my head. "What was she on?"

"I guess she felt comfortable with me. Hey, I enjoyed her too. But after hearing about her four children, I knew I was smiling only until the night was over. All we didn't do in that night was not gonna get done. She was attractive and all, with a beautiful waistline to have four kids. But I don't even want to date her because she appears to be the type of person ya could fall in love with." He paused. "So what's dude's name, and when will ya see him again?"

"His name is Melvin, and I don't know when I will see him again. I liked him so much that I would love to see him again as soon as tonight. I believe God heard my mother's prayers and felt my frustration." I paused. "When you don't have a man for some reason everybody thinks it is because you don't want one. I just let them think whatever."

"Look at ya! Ya a gorgeous woman, but almost 40. There is somethin' wrong! And instead of placing it on the men ya have had in ya lifetime, people assume it must be because ya not ready. Look at how long ya have lived and the men ya have come in contact with. Where else should the blame go? You and I had a perfect relationship years ago, I thought, and all of a sudden ya got tired and needed space. And what about that guy name Gary? Now he was a cool cat from what ya told me. Then there was Brad, I mean this fellow looked like a supermodel. What was with him? Nothing from what ya told me, and I can go on."

"Let's not go there." I raised my hand telling Mike to stop. "I had my reasons. But this guy Melvin is different. I can feel it. I think I can really get into him. I really do. Don't look at me like that. I'm serious." Mike didn't believe me.

"Well, I will believe it when I see it. I will say this much, ya did have a glow on ya face that I have not seen in quite some time. Plus ya have never danced with one guy the entire night, so maybe he stands a chance. I hope so because sometimes ya can be so finicky." He paused and then he continued. "Why did you all dance slow the entire night — even off of the fast songs?"

"He can't dance fast, so even though we stayed on the floor we kept it slow so that he would feel comfortable."

"Oh, I wondered what was going on. He made me laugh when he hit this little move like the Four Tops. I tried to hold my laugh in until that point. When he did that, I almost died laughing." We both giggled.

"I have to get up from here, Boo and go home to take a shower. Breakfast was great as usual. When I get rich I am going to hire you as my chef. I have to get home, so I can call this man! Maybe he will change his plans for the summer now that he has met me. I don't have four kids under ten." I said humorously as I pushed my chair up to the table. I kissed Mike on his cheek as he smiled up at me, and then I ran upstairs to get dressed.

When I pulled into my parking lot, Stacy sat on her porch. Cameron was probably gone to work. His car wasn't in his parking space. Stacy couldn't wait for me to get out of the car. She watched me the entire time it took me to park. Once I walked toward the porch she and I spoke to each other at the same time with a hand gesture and a smile.

She followed me once I got onto the porch. "Hey, girl. You stayed out last night, huh?" Stacy asked.

"Yeah, Mike's house. He and I went out last night, and I was too tired to come home." I stuck the key in my lock to unlock my door. Stacy stood right behind me. "Come on in." I said as I slung the door open. If I didn't say come in, she would have come in anyway. That was just her way.

"Girl, you know Cameron and I are talking about taking a vacation."

"Oh, yeah, that's good. Where are you going?"

"I don't know. Cameron wants to go and see his darn mother. His mother lives in California. I always wanted to go to California but not to see his darn mother. Girrrrl, his mother gets on my nerves! And I don't think she really tries. She's just messed up that way." Stacy flopped down on the living room sofa, and I sat on the loveseat across from her. I picked up the remote to the stereo and cut on some soft music.

"What bothers you so much about her or should I say what bothers her so much about you?"

"She has this thing about her baby. Cameron ain't no baby! Doesn't she see all those muscles in that man's chest? Does she think I am with him to ride up and down on the rollercoaster? That's a grown man, honey. I am ridin' the rollercoaster all right. One that she can't get on."

I giggled. "Girl, you are crazy."

"See, he is the seventh child, and he isn't the youngest. Her youngest child passed away with pneumonia at the age of 20 about five years ago. Ever since then, his mother has been overprotected about Cameron. She lives for her children. Really lives for her children. I think she worries about Cameron most because all of her other children live in the same city as she does. When I went to their last family reunion she followed Cameron and me around all day. She made sure I cut the ends off of his bread for his rib sandwich, put paprika on his potato salad, and put ice in his beer like she knows he likes it."

"Uhhhh, Cameron likes ice in his beer? That's nasty!" I was disgusted thinking about ice in beer.

"Yeah, but that's Cameron. When she lived in D.C. and we visited her, she would remake our bed after I had already made it up. She cooked all Cameron's favorite foods while we were there. I got so sick watching her cater to him. I was ready to go before it was time for us to go." Stacy put her finger down her throat and made a gagging sound.

"Well, California sounds good to me. I would go, and I would not let the way his mother treats him bother me. Stay busy by staying out of her house. Have fun, girl! You allow her to take care of Cameron and give you a break. You go shopping and touring. Get you a massage or something. You've never been to California, so go and enjoy yourself. Let her have her baby. You have him all the time when you are here. You're trivializing things again."

"Yeah, you're right. I didn't think about it like that. But anyway, if we go I am going to leave you a key to the house to check on Poo-Poo. If you don't mind. I will show you where her food is and everything. If you can or when you can, spend a little time with Poo-Poo for me. Rub her a minute or two. She knows where to use it when I am gone."

I cut my eyes at Stacy. I didn't want to spend time with a cat, especially not Poo-Poo. "I will try. But honey, I am not making any promises to spend time with Poo-Poo. She has never liked me anyway, and you know that. I still remember the last time her butt scratched me! I wanted to scratch her back, but I was too afraid." I turned my head away from Stacy.

"She likes you. Poo is just a real woman in a cat's body. She gets funny sometimes. Don't mind old Poo. I swear she has a period because at a certain time of the month she doesn't like me either. She will only let Cameron rub on her."

"How long will you be gone when you do leave?"

"A week at the most. But I will let you know for sure at least two weeks before we leave. Well, let me get over here and get this man's dinner ready because if I don't have it ready he might call his mammy on me. And I don't want that because we might end up where she is for our vacation." Stacy chuckled.

"You didn't call that man's mother a mammy. You are a mess, girl."

We both stood to our feet and walked to the door. "I'm going to cook some cabbage and fried chicken. You want me to cook enough for you?" Stacy asked as she held the front door open.

"You know you don't have to ask." I never turned down any food. Well, if I looked at you and you didn't look clean, I might. But food was very serious for me. Food and I were in love. At times food could be the best man ever.

"I didn't know whether you were going to be

here or not."

"I'll be here. I'll probably roll out later on tonight."

"Okay, I'll bring your plate over when I'm done. See ya." Stacy walked out of the door.

"Bye crazy woman. Poo better be good to me while you all are on vacation. You tell her that too." I pointed my finger and laughed. "Or you will come back and find Poo taped up on your stereo."

Stacy laughed. "You betta not hurt my cat. She ain't don nothin' to you."

"Yes, she did. Scratched me, ol' cranky cat. Get her some Midol!" I laughed as I closed my door.

Now it was time to take a shower and relax. But first I checked my answering machine to see if I had any important messages.

Answering machine:

"Hey, Demisha, this is Mike. Where are ya, Baby-girl? We have a lunch date, don't stand me up again." Beep.

"Hey, baby, this is mama. Call mama when ya get home. I love ya." Beep.

"Hey, Demisha. You sound just as lovely on your answering machine as you do in person. This is Melvin. Call me when you get in." Beep. A huge grin took over my face. I was happy to hear that he was just as interested in me as I was in him.

"Hi, Demisha. It's Rick. Call me. I haven't heard from you. Is something wrong? If it's that foot thing, I got it under control. Mama bought that good foot powder this time. Call me." Beep. The machine rewound the tape.

I flopped down in the chair next to the phone and reached over for my purse. I searched it to make sure I still had Melvin's number safely put away. I took it out of my purse and looked at it a minute. Then I picked up the phone and dialed Melvin's number. The phone rang, and I got butterflies like a teenage girl listening to it ring.

"Hello." A man with a deep voice answered. I was certain it was Melvin, although he sounded a little different over the phone.

"Hello, may I please speak with Melvin?" Although I was a teacher, I could be Southern sometimes. But whenever I talked to a man I liked, I put on my teacher voice. My teacher voice was proper and from New York.

"This is he, love. So you finally called me back."

"Are you cognizant of who you are conversing with?"

"Of course I am. This is Demisha. I wouldn't normally say this, but I have been waiting on your call. I called you earlier this morning just to say good morning to you." His voice embodied sexiness. It sent chills up my spine.

"I got your message. I was over my friend's house. I was too tired last night to drive home. I should say earlier this morning because it was morning when we left the club—about one."

"The guy who you were with?"

"Yes. He is my best friend. There is nothing between us." I reassured him. I didn't want to lose him before I reeled him in.

"Well, I'm sure of that because of the way you two acted at the club. I think it's great that you can have that kind of friendship with a man. I have never been able to have a female as a close friend. I do have some as friends. That's great—your friendship."

"Yes, it is. I love Mike. He is the best friend anyone could have. So you called me this morning to say good morning to me, how thoughtful."

"I do what I feel. I knew that you were probably tired because we left the club late. But I really wanted to see could I have convinced you to come out and have breakfast with me. I wanted to ask you while we were at the club, but I didn't want to seem too pushy. I just had such a great time with you, and I couldn't stop thinking about you." Sincerity filled his voice. He melted my heart as I listened to him talk.

"I thought about you too."

"Oh, yeah."

"Yes, I thought about you." I giggled.

"Well, do you think you might want to see me tonight?"

I smiled from ear to ear. "I don't know. I might."

"Well, I promise you that you will have a lovely time. Now that's a promise, and I keep my promises." He assured me.

"How can a lady turn down a man who keeps his promises? I will be ready by 8:00. Is that okay?"

"Why of course. Where should I pick you up?"

"I don't know. I would have you come to my

house, but you might be some kind of murder." I said humorously, but I was very serious. I didn't allow men to come to my house until I was comfortable with them, which took months usually.

"No love, as good as you look, I promise I won't kill you. I won't do that unless I do it with kisses." He smoothly bounced off his tongue. There was something about this man. I could feel it in my bones, and my bones didn't lie.

"Well, tell me where you plan to take me, and I'll decide where we will meet."

"My place — only if it is okay with you. I promise you more than a wonderful time. I will not do anything to disrespect you. I love to treat a lady like a queen."

"Where is your place?"

"I live in Marietta off of 75 North."

"Well, why don't I come to you? Give me the directions."

"That's lovely."

"I must warn you that I will tell my friend where I am going just in case you turn out to be a maniac."

"Okay, that's fine with me as long as I have the

pleasure of your company tonight."

"You're such a good talker. I don't know if I should trust you."

"You can trust me—I promise. I just feel something special about you. You're one of a kind. I can tell. I don't know why you haven't been snatched up."

"Yes, I am one of a kind. I don't allow men to snatch me up. I will only be snatched up by the right man, and it takes a lot to be right for me."

"Okay, so you are letting me know that I have my work cut out for me. No problem. I love challenges. I am the man for the challenge. If there is a pole to climb, I will climb it."

"We'll see if your talk is cheap or highly qualified for the mission."

****

I dressed in a simple pink short tank dress that fitted my body from top to bottom with a sheer shawl to go around my shoulders. I wore sandals that had straps to cross up my calves. They had six-inch heels—accented my legs perfectly. I painted my toes with garnet colored polish and one coat of clear on top to give them that sparkle. I put my hair up in a roll and left three spiraled curls hanging. My makeup was flawless and my legs as smooth as a baby's bottom.

The directions he gave me were simple. I stood at his door at eight o'clock on the dot. I primped a little before I rung his doorbell. I was very nervous. His home was huge from the outside. He lived in a newly developed subdivision that had a sign stating the starting price for the homes in that area was $550,000. I thought to myself, how lucky could a girl get at a nightclub.

The door opened. "Hi, come on in. So you found the place without having a problem I see." Melvin said.

"Atlanta is my home, and I have been to every city surrounding it as well. Your home is lovely." It was huge and beautifully decorated with very high ceilings.

"Why thank you. I must confess that I didn't decorate it myself. My mother helped me with some of it. She loves decorating."

"Where does your mother live?" I hoped she didn't live in the same house with him.

"She lives in Washington — the state. One day you must accompany me when I visit her. You can walk in front of me; just follow the rose petals once we get in the den." I knew he wanted to check me out from the back. I didn't hesitate to walk in front of him because the back view was just as good as the front.

"Rose petals? How sweet!" The rose petals led us into his dining room where the table was set elegantly. The lights were dimmed and candles were lit. "Now this is gorgeous. I love your dining room set. It's just enough for you, but it's beautiful!" This man or his mother had exquisite taste.

"You can sit here." He said as he pulled out my chair.

"Why thank you."

"I will be right back with dinner. I prepared it all myself. I hope you like it."

"I love everything so far. I'm almost positive I will love dinner."

"Be right back."

It was surreal. I had never been on a date so wonderful, and it was only 5 minutes into the date. This man had already swept me off of my feet, which was something many men couldn't do.

Melvin rolled into the dining room a silver serving tray. "I forgot to ask you exactly what you wanted to eat. So I prepared my favorites: mushroom covered steak in my special sauce, onion marinated potatoes, Caesar salad, and garlic bread with a touch of cheese." He uncovered each dish as he announced it.

I thought I was in heaven. This was Mr. Right, and I felt it in my toes. I only hoped that he could feel that I was Ms. Right.

"Okay, now I shall take my seat here. Oh, hold on I forgot the wine!" He jumped up from his chair to get the wine. I could see him in the kitchen from the dining room.

He came back into the dining room with the wine. "Okay, I am back to accompany my princess of beauty. May I kiss your hand? I must kiss your hand." He reached his hand out, and I put my hand in his. He kissed my hand softly.

"You can't keep spoiling me with such wonderful treatment unless you are going to continue to do it. I am the kind of woman that spoils very easily."

"Well, let me spoil you." He said. I smiled.

"Did you buy this food cooked already?" I smirked. "You actually cooked all this yourself?"

He smiled. "Why of course I cooked it myself. What I don't do myself you will be sure to know. How is it?" He watched me eat.

"I think it's great. The salad — everything is unbelievable. You cook better than I do on my good days."

"So what are you saying, you're not a good cook? Are you trying to tell me that just in case I'm looking for a woman to cook?" He awaited my answer.

I smiled. "No, I know with you cooking like this, you do not need a cook. Your mother has taught you well."

He giggled. "Smart girl. Yes, she has. I love to cook. It's a part of me. So what did your friend say about me? I'm sure he gave you his thoughts about me, especially since you two are great friends."

"No, he didn't. He could tell that I sort of liked you, but he had nothing else to say at that moment."

"That's a good sign. A good sign that you will be taken with me and will someday be my wife." He looked me in my eyes and dropped his smile. He didn't bat an eye or budge.

I was stuck. He was good at seducing my mind. He worked from the inside out. Finally my eyes blinked, and I spoke. "Oh, please. Is that what you are looking for? Have you ever been married?" My heart was beating fast. He really rattled my nerves when he mentioned marriage. His words pierced my heart. It was kind of scary, but I gathered my composure quickly. I didn't want to let him see me sweat.

"Oh, me, yes. But I do want to get married again. I have been married only once. My ex-wife and I stayed married ten years."

"No, you are kidding, ten years! You married young?"

"Well, I married my ex-wife when I was 20 years old, and she was 27 years old."

"You love older women?"

"Never purposely, it just happens that way as you can see. I just like what I like. I like a woman who has me sprung from the beginning."

My eyes got bigger. "Oh my, sprung did you say?"

"Yes, totally into her as a person. I have been divorced now for four years, and you're the first woman that has ever had me sprung from the beginning. I am totally into you. What man in his right mind wouldn't be? So what do you do for a living?"

"I thought I told you that I was a teacher, Mr. Sprung. If you are so sprung, how did you forget that? I'm a teacher. I have been teaching for seventeen years now — different grades. Now I am finally teaching the age group I have always wanted to teach, first graders. The sweet 7- year-old students."

"How nice. Myself, I sell everything from household appliances all the way to cars. I own my own business."

"It figures a salesman — smooth talker. You have all the right words to say and a hypnotic gaze."

He giggled. "Yeah, yeah, but I promise you that I will never lead you astray. I am very sincere. I don't sell my customers any old thing. I don't run my business out of my car, so I have to be there to face people the next day. I'm a good man. You'll see."

"Any kids?"

"Um huh, I am not the only one with a faulty memory I see or are you testing me? Remember, I told you that I didn't have any. No kids. My ex-wife and I never had any kids. I used to be sad about it but not anymore."

I shook my head from side to side. "You're almost too good to be true. You're something else Melvin."

"No, Demisha you are!" We laughed.

****

"I'll clear the table later. Let's go to my room and dance like we did last night." He stood up from the table.

"Your room!" I was shocked by his boldness. I stood to my feet and removed the cloth napkin from my lap. "I didn't come here to go to your room." Yet, I never resisted.

"I won't do anything you don't want me to do, I promise." He said softly as he held his hand out for mine.

Oh, God, what does that mean? I thought to myself. I might just want him to do everything — the night is going so well. I will be okay. I will control myself. He led me to his room.

His bedroom was gigantic. He had a king size bed, a sitting area with a full bronze plush sofa, a fireplace, and still plenty of room for us to dance. The wall of his room was some type of elegant bronze textured material. His bed was covered in burgundy satin sheets and a burgundy and gold duvet. Sheer material looped across the tall, wide cherry wood bed poles. There were glass French doors near the windows that opened up to the balcony. The moonlight shined through the doors. It was beautiful. The view had secretly undressed me. I magnetically walked over to the French doors.

While I watched the moon illumine the sky, the music began to play. I turned around toward him. "So may I have this dance?" He asked. I smiled and embraced him.

We danced as Freddie Jackson's *You Are My Lady* filled the room with passion. I was still in awe because this was unbelievable. This was the way a woman should feel all the time. As we danced I could feel him breathe on my neck as if he wanted to kiss it. Just as I felt his breath, I felt a soft peck on my neck from his soothing lips. I don't think he was fully aware of what his lips had done.

"You are so beautiful and sexy. I have never wanted a woman as bad as I want you right now." He whispered into my ear. I said nothing although I felt the same way he did. "May I kiss your lips? Please, Demisha." He brought his head around and looked into my eyes. I couldn't resist his beautiful brown eyes. He was so kind — so polite.

"Yes, I would love that." I responded as I closed my eyes. He kissed my lips, and as he French kissed me I began to melt in his arms. This man was a remarkable kisser. Surely he was making love to me already.

He didn't stop at kissing my lips. He moved down and kissed my shoulder as he rubbed my back. His hands flowed from my back to my butt, lifting my dress a little.

"I want you, Demisha. I don't think it's wrong to want you now. Do you?" He whispered softly into my ear. This man was overpowering me without physically overpowering me.

Oh, how I wanted to take my time with him. He was a keeper. I wanted to say no, but I didn't because the heat of my body said yes. "Will you respect me in the morning?" I asked him.

"Of course I will. I'm a gentleman." He kissed me and then he continued. "I know we are two consenting adults. I won't hold you to anything. You can tell me stop whenever you want to."

"I want you too. Take me." And he took me just as I asked. He lifted me up off my feet and carried me over to his bed. Laying me gently down on the side that was near the French doors, I could see the dark sky and the moonlight. He untied my shoes and everywhere the long straps loosened, he kissed.

"It feels so good." I moaned with continuous movement of my head as he kissed in between my thighs. He took his time with me. The moon danced in the sky. Out of all my 37 years I had never felt so good in my life. It was more than just good sex. There was something else I felt. I knew Melvin felt it too.

I awoke the next morning from the sound of Melvin's footsteps as he brought a breakfast tray into the room. "Good morning, sleepyhead. You were tired. You like pancakes? I hope you do." He put the tray on the bed where I lay.

"Of course I do. You were not lying when you said you wouldn't stop spoiling me." I sat up in the bed.

"No, I wasn't. You're beautiful in the morning." He kissed my forehead.

"Thank you." I slid the tray closer to me.

"May I have a kiss?" He asked.

"No! I haven't brushed my teeth yet."

"That's okay for the woman I am going to marry someday." He leaned up against me and tried to kiss me again.

"No." I pushed him away playfully.

"Okay, but next time I won't accept no."

"My mother would die if she knew what I had done with you. She is a Christian woman."

"I won't tell her if you won't."

"Do you have to work today?"

"I work on my own time, that's the best thing about being a salesman and having your own business. Can we spend today together if you have nothing to do?"

"I haven't called my mother. She will be worried about me."

"Call her from here. I can't let you go now. You might not come back. The phone works. I thought about unplugging them and kidnapping you. But I said nah, it's too soon for that. Maybe the second date." We giggled.

"I have a cell phone. You are funny. Don't scare me away."

"So did you like last night?"

"Yes, I enjoyed last night. You're quite a romantic man. I can tell it comes naturally to you. I like that."

"Was it as good as I promised it would be?"

"Indeed it was. It was very good. I just might call you Mel now." We both laughed.

"You are so wonderful. You're strong, yet you have a wonderful sense of humor. So far I love everything I have seen about you."

"Well, I hope you will say that a month or two from now."

"You can't be that bad."

"I'm not, but I can't be all that good either."

"Please. When you finish will you shower with me?"

"I might. Why are you so confident? You just ask me whatever you want to ask me like it is something I supposed to do."

"I know you like me just as much as I like you. I can feel it. So why play games? I ask with confidence because I feel your confidence in what we have."

"What we have! What do we have? We just met."

"Yeah, but you know it's right. You try to play cool to protect your feelings. I can feel your energy oozing from your body. You want me just as bad as I want you. You're hoping I am the right man for you just like I am hoping you're the right woman for me. Well, I know you're right. Time has to catch up I guess."

Enthralled with his words, I changed the subject. "Breakfast is delicious. I love to eat. I really should be overweight the way I love to eat. That may be something you won't like about me." I rambled.

"No, like I told you, I love to cook. So what is better for a person that loves to cook than having someone around who loves to eat?" He lifted the tray up from me and pulled the covers away. He led me by my hand toward the bathroom. "I noticed how you changed the subject. You are going to have to face your feelings soon. I will give you time to do that."

"I don't have on any clothes!" He pulled on me.

"And there is no one here but us. I already saw that beautiful body you have. Besides, you would just take them off anyway once we got to the shower."

"Oh, Mel, you are so charismatic." He stopped and turned towards me and hugged me.

"You called me Mel without thinking about it, and it sounded so good." He was happy.

After our shower, Mel literally dressed me in some of his clothes. He washed my underwear with his hands. I looked really cute dressed in Mel's silk shirt and slacks that he cuffed slightly to fit me. I felt like things were moving too fast, but I didn't want to slow them down.

"That shall hold you until I buy you something to wear." He said as he finished the last cuff and stood up and kissed my lips. "Sorry, I had no shoes for you, but pink always looks good with sky blue and gray." He laughed. "You will be fine. We will get you something from the mall before we start the day."

Mel and I spent most of the day out. It was as if we had known each other for years. He was affectionate, and he pampered me. He trusted me, and I trusted him.

We didn't get back to Mel's house until about eight o'clock that night, and Mel still didn't want me to leave. I didn't want to leave either. I had the best time of my life with him. He held me as we stood at my car about fifteen minutes. He begged me to spend one more night with him.

"Don't do this to me, Mel. You know that I want to stay, but I must go. I haven't called my mother since I have been here, and I promised her that we would go to lunch or dinner tomorrow. I must go even though I want to stay."

"Okay, I guess I will let you go. I have to. Don't I? I told you I should just kidnap you and call it a day." He teased. He opened my car door. I got inside of the car. Mel watched as I pulled away.

As I rode the interstate I thought about Mel. I could still feel his wonderful kisses on my body. I shivered at the thought. I never believed in love at first sight, but Mel changed all of that for me. And what really made me feel good was that he was just as crazy about me as I was about him. Mel actually neutralized my strong, cocky, nonchalant attitude. He made me seem as if I was sweet as pie. I didn't want to sleep with Mel the first night that we were together because I liked him so much. But I was under his spell.

I felt as if I loved Mel. And it seemed silly to me to feel that way so soon, but I did. A 37 year-old woman was supposed to know better. But Mel seduced my heart. I knew Mel was the one for me because I actually felt guilty about having sex with him. Mel made me feel worth more than a one-night stand.

When I got home it was a little after nine. Stacy looked out of her window as I pulled up. Before I could turn my car off, she was outside of her house waiting on the porch. She tapped her foot on the porch like a mother ready to unleash her wrath on her disobedient child.

"Tell me about your date that you put my cabbage plate in the refrigerator for." Stacy said as I approached the porch.

"Girl, let me at least get on the porch please!" I retorted.

"And what's this you have on? You didn't leave with these things on. I'm no fool, girl. I want the gossip because I know there is some!" Her hands rested on her hips, and she poked out her lips.

"Stacy, where is your husband? I need him to come and get your crazy tail!"

"He won't come because he knows I want the gossip. I have got to get the news about this date that kept you out twenty-four hours." When I opened my door she followed me inside.

"Stacy, you are crazy."

"There is something different about you, Demisha. You are glowing, girl. You have a certain air about you!" She flopped on my sofa.

I smiled. "What do you mean I have an air about me?"

"Don't try to fool me, Ms. Thang. I have been living next door to you too long. You never came home in different clothes — new clothes at that. They don't look cheap either. And if you were with Mike you would have been home by morning, so give me the scoop, the scooooop!" She bounced up and down on the sofa anxiously.

"Okay, Stacy, okay! Would you like something to drink?"

"Noooo! I already placed my order. I want the scoop!"

"I think I want something to drink." I poured me a glass of ice tea.

"Give me some too. I changed my mind."

"I thought you didn't want anything to drink."

"Well, if you are going to waste time to pour you some, you might as well pour me some too. I just said I didn't want any so you could get right to the news."

"Nosy."

"Hey, I never denied who I am."

After I poured our tea, Stacy came into the kitchen, and we sat at the table. She didn't take her eyes off of me. I began to tell her about my night out with Mel. "Okay, it's true that I have met someone special." I took another sip of my tea which infuriated Stacy. She wanted me to tell her everything without taking a breath if I could manage it.

"I know you did. I know! It was great wasn't it? You have that glow, girl. Look at you!" She was excited.

I was excited too, but I tried to hold my composure. Then it was over. In one breath I let it go. "Ahhhh! It was great, Stacy! I feel like I am 18 years old again, and I have met the first love of my life. He's so wonderful, Stacy! Really wonderful! I just met him Saturday night at the club with Mike. I danced the entire night with him. I didn't give anyone else a dance! Not even Mike and usually we dance one dance together before we leave the club. He called me the morning after the club, but I wasn't home. He wanted to take me to breakfast. When I returned his call he asked me to dinner. And that's how your cabbage plate ended up in the refrigerator. He prepared dinner for me at his house! Girl, his house is lovely! When he greeted me at his door he looked so sexy and relaxed. He wore a silver silky looking big collar shirt and gray slacks. Just gorgeous from head to toe! He has such a beautiful body, not too big or too small. Not too muscular but tone and cut like a body should be. His kisses melted me literally in his arms. I actually felt faint when his lips caressed mine. Girl, he is so wonderful that I'm scared he won't be mine. I have been so messed up to men, breaking their hearts. I feel like I don't deserve him. You understand what I am saying, Stacy? Stacy?" I don't think I took a breath. Stacy was in a daze; her eyes were all dreamy as if she was the one newly in love. "Stacy, where are you?" I shook her arm.

"Girl, I was stuck on the good kisses. I like a man that knows how to kiss. I'm sorry. I was just trying to imagine him. Everything seems so beautiful, like a fairy tale. Did you have sex with him? Well, I know you did, but I will be nice and ask you. Details, details please!" She waved her hands impatiently in the air.

"Yes, Stacy we made love." I said disgusted with myself because I didn't want Mel to think I was some easy lay.

"Made love, what is this? Usually it's have sex! Oh, girl, you're in deep. This man has you!"

"Girl, he made my body feel like heaven! It was amazing! I have never felt this way before. I can't even begin to tell you how many men I have been with and still never have I felt this way! Girl, he didn't want me to leave. He bought these clothes for me so that I could spend the day with him. He washed my underwear on his hands, girl! How many men will do that?" I squeezed Stacy's hand and smiled looking up toward the ceiling.

Stacy had a huge smile on her face. "Uuuuuh you stankin' heifer! You just enjoyed yourself. I hope this is your husband! I really do. You've been by yourself far too long. I will be praying for you."

"Thank you, Stace. I need all the prayer I can get. I am ready for a husband! This man was made for me, I tell you. He makes my hard tail as soft as a pillow, and I love it. I know my mother would disagree with me having sex with him, but she doesn't know about all the other sex I've had." We laughed.

"Your mother is only Christian, girl. She isn't stupid. You are not fooling her. If she is like my mother, she is probably just praying for your wild tail to calm down and meet the right man! All mothers want the best for their daughters. He must really be the one because you wouldn't normally care about how soon you had sex."

The phone rang. "Let me get this, girl. You should be in bed with your husband anyway." I walked toward the kitchen phone. "Hello." I answered the phone.

"Hey, baby. I just wanted to make sure you got home safely." Mel said on the other end. I turned toward Stacy with a big smile on my face.

"Yes, Mel I'm home. My neighbor is here. Can I call you back as soon as I put her out?" I giggled.

"Sure, baby." He said.

"Okay, I'll call you back." I hung up the phone. "You have got to get out, Stacy. Cameron is calling you, honey."

"That man is Mr. Right. I can feel it! So long to all those Mr. Rightnows. This is not an average relationship for you girl, and I am happy for you. I hope he makes you happy like Cameron makes me happy — sometimes anyway. Well, that's marriage, but I love my baby. Let me go before you actually throw me out. I see how you are looking at me. Give me hug." Stacy hugged me. "I am really happy for you, Demisha. Don't ruin this because you're afraid. You will have your problems, but it will be okay, girl. Pray about it." Stacy said on a serious note. I locked the door behind her.

As I walked back to the kitchen table I stopped and smiled. Glee took over me. I sat down at the kitchen table and stared in space. I thought about Mel. I knew Mel was Mr. Right because my heart automatically opened up for him. That's how I always thought love should be. I never wanted love by trying to love. Love should be there, and with Mel it was. With all the other guys love would have been too much like work — hard work.

I didn't really feel like praying. I guess because I never lived my life right, and I thought God wouldn't really want to listen to me. But I prayed anyway. I prayed that Mel was my husband that God had just for me. I don't know if God heard me, but I prayed. I was tempted not to because I had copulated with Mel. How could I ask God to bless something that I had started wrong? I guess somewhere I had faith that God could make it right.

I called Mel back after I prayed. He came over later that night and stayed. It seemed he missed me even though I had just left him. Before Mel and I turned in, I called my mother and reassured her of our lunch date for the next day. She had a million questions for me about where I had been for two days without calling her and without answering my cell phone. I told her we would talk about it when I saw her. I got rid of her by saying I had to use the bathroom. After I hung up with my mother, Mike called me.

"Hey, what's up? Haven't heard from ya, Baby-girl." Mike said.

"Mike, let me call you tomorrow. Mel is here."

"Mel. Who in the world is Mel?"

"The guy from the club Saturday night."

"Oh. I thought his name was Melvin. Ya call him Mel now? Ya must know him a little better since the club?" Mike giggled. He knew me well.

I laughed. "Funny. Well, you knooow." I said smiling as I looked at Mel.

"I'll call ya tomorrow, love ya." Mike said.

"Love you too, bye." I hung up the phone.

"Who was that? Mike?" Mel asked.

"Yes."

"Do you talk about everything with him?" Mel played with my hair.

"Of course, Mike and I don't have secrets. He knows me just as well as a female best friend would know me. And I know him just as a man best friend would know him. We don't hide anything from each other, and we talk about everything that you can imagine."

"I guess that's a great feeling."

"I must tell you that Mike and I were once involved. Awhile ago—it didn't work out."

"Why not? It seems as if you two would be perfect for each other since you are such great friends."

"Well, not exactly. I am not and wasn't ever physically attractive to Mike. But he is a great person, and that is the reason we are best friends now. We dated two years, and after we ended the relationship we have been platonic friends ever since."

"So has it been strictly platonic since the day you guys said it was over?"

"Yes, it has. I wouldn't lie to you."

"So, I have nothing to worry about?" He smirked. His eyes pierced my soul for the truth.

"Of course not." I answered seriously.

"Tell me, did you ever tell him why things didn't work?"

"Well, maybe I have one secret he doesn't

know. No, I would never hurt Mike like that. He is wonderful, and I could never replace what we have as friends. He would say little things that implied that he sort of knew, but then we just went on with our lives."

"Come on. Let's go upstairs. I need to get out of these clothes and into a bath so that you can bathe me." Mel said as he pulled me in his arms and began to walk toward the stairs.

"This is my place. How do you know which way to go?"

"I don't, but I want you to show me."

CHAPTER TWO

TIME TO MEET THE FAMILY

Six months later

Mel hosted my family's Thanksgiving dinner. Normally we spent it at my mother's house or my aunt Kissy's house. But Mel wanted to meet everyone, and he decided hosting Thanksgiving dinner would be the perfect way. Mel had already met my mother. He took her to lunch every other weekend after meeting her. She loved Mel instantly. When Mike got to know Mel, they got along well also. He and Mike often talked on the phone to each other and worked on car projects together. My mother and my best friend loved Mel, and now it was time for all the others to meet him.

Mel and I cooked Thanksgiving dinner together. He cooked a few dishes my family wasn't accustomed to having on Thanksgiving. I didn't worry about how my family would take to the unusual dishes of food because everything Mel prepared was delicious. He was a terrific cook, and my family loved eating. Mel and I worked hard to have everything perfect.

"So, what do you think your family will say?" Mel asked as we stood in the kitchen preparing the food.

"Baby, they are going to love it. Don't worry. They're just happy that I'm happy and that they can finally meet the man my mother has been bragging about. Although you will have to explain these dishes you made them, everything will be fine. I think a non-traditional Thanksgiving dinner is wonderful. I never liked chitterlings anyway. My aunt Kissy is a character. She might want you to write down the recipes for some of these dishes." I landed a kiss on Mel's lips.

"I will not mind giving her the recipes as long as I can have her niece. She can have the house if she wants!" Mel smiled and lifted me up into the air.

"Babe, put me down. They should be here soon. Mike is bringing my mother, so they should be here in the next ten minutes or so. Mike is just like my mother, never late. Let me check the dining room table."

Mel and I bought—well Mel bought a new dining room table set just to accommodate my family for Thanksgiving. I accompanied him and picked it out.

"You told me not to worry, but how many times are you going to check the table? Can the table do something I am not aware of?" Mel walked behind me.

"I just want to make sure everything is perfect, but I am not worried."

"You know that's why I love you; you make sure everything is perfect."

"Not perfect but as close to perfect as things can get."

As we stood looking at the dining room table the doorbell rang. Ding-dong. "The doorbell! I'll get it." I said as Mel went in the opposite direction.

Mel was nervous, and I knew he probably went to the bathroom to check his appearance. I looked out the window near the door and there stood my mother and Mike.

I opened the door with a huge smile. "You guys made it! Come on in, mama. Who is this, Mike?" I asked. Mike had a date with him. No one I had seen before. She was pretty, but a little thicker than usual.

"This is my date Carla." Mike answered.

"Hi, Carla. I'm Demisha, Mike's best friend." I smiled and gave her a hug out of nervous energy.

"It's very nice meeting you, Demisha. I have heard some wonderful things about you. Your home is gorgeous." Carla said.

I blushed from ear to ear. "Well, it's not mine yet I should tell you. It's my boyfriend's home. He's something else. Come on guys and follow me." I led them into the living room.

"Oh, this house is beautiful, this living room is huge." My mother said as she looked around. And then she leaned in and whispered to me, "Calm down. Everything is going to go well." She kissed my cheek.

"I love the high ceilings." Mike added.

"You guys have a seat, and I will bring you out some drinks." I put some soft jazz on before I left the room.

Mel helped me get the drinks together, and he carried them out. "Hello, everyone. Hey, Mother." Mel said as he set the tray of drinks on the table and kissed my mother's cheek. "This is fresh lemonade, none of that powdered stuff." Everyone laughed. "Okay I know mother and Mike. But I don't know you. Is this your guest, Mike?" Mel walked over towards the sofa that

Mike and Carla sat on.

"Yes, this is my date Carla. And Carla this is my friend Mel, Demisha's boyfriend." Mike said.

"Okay, it is very nice to meet you, Carla. Mike's a great guy. I'm Mel, Demisha's fiancé." Everyone turned and looked at me. I got strangled a little as I drank my lemonade, shocked at Mel calling me his fiancé.

I started coughing.

"Baby, are ya okay?" My mother asked.

"I am fine. I'm fine. Lemonade just went down the wrong way." I said.

"Oh, man, when did y'all decide to make that move?" Mike asked.

My mother was gleaming, and I was speechless because Mel had not mentioned anything to me about marriage. I didn't know I was his fiancé.

"Oh, I'm so happy for you two!" My mother said as she put her hand over her mouth and her eyes teared up.

Mel looked at me, and I looked at him. He walked over to me, and he wrapped his arms around me. "Demisha Coleman, would you please be my wife?" Mel dropped on one knee. He looked directly into my eyes. I could hear my mother crying with joy, but at that moment it seemed as if everyone else in the room had disappeared. And it was only Mel and I.

"I, I, I don't know what to say." I stuttered. I was elated but in shock.

"Say yes, baby. Say yes!" I heard my mother say from the sideline.

"Of course the answer is yes. Yes!" I screamed as I wrapped my arms around his neck. Mel took out a ring box from his pocket and opened it up. He stood to his feet. Inside was a beautiful three carat diamond engagement ring. When I say beautiful, I mean beautiful. The diamonds sparkled from Atlanta to New York. I felt like a movie star. He took my hand and put the ring on my finger as my hand shook tremendously.

"I am just shocked guys because Mel never led on about this. I didn't know a thing." I sniffed with tears running down my face.

"Well, I knew all the time." Mike smiled and stood up and hugged Mel and I.

"No! You knew, and you didn't tell me! Mike!" I said in disbelief.

"I can keep a secret, Baby-girl. It was hard because ya my girl, but now Mel is family too. And I had to honor his wishes." Mike defended himself.

"No one told me. What did ya think I couldn't

keep a secret?" My mother giggled and cried at the same time.

"Well, Mother I wanted it to be just as shocking to you as it was for her. I like surprising people. You had already given me your blessings many times. So I knew you wouldn't mind having me as a son-in-law." Mel said.

Carla stood up and congratulated us too. It was just a happy moment filled with emotions. The doorbell rang again. Ding-dong. "It's the door! It's the door!" I said as my mother took her tissue and wiped my eyes.

"I'll get it." Mike volunteered.

"I'm sorry we are crying all over the place, Carla." I apologized.

"No, no, this is a happy occasion. I understand. I am about to cry myself." Carla said.

Mike led my other family members into the living room.

"Hello, everyone! Sorry we are late." My aunt Kissy May said. There were hellos going everywhere.

"Why is everyone crying?" My cousin Barbara observed.

"Mel just asked Demisha to marry him." Mike boasted.

"Oh, God! That's wonderful!" Aunt Kissy May said as she walked over to me.

"I'm sorry everyone, let me go wipe my eyes, and then we will continue." I said. I was so emotional that I couldn't introduce Mel to my family. I walked to the bathroom, and I saw Mel follow me. I pushed the lid down on the toilet and sat down for a brief moment.

Mel bent down in front of me. "Baby, this is really emotional for you, huh?" He put his arm around me.

"Mel, this is the happiest moment in my life, and never did I think it would be this soon. I am so blessed to have a man like you. God really loves my mother because it had to be her prayers that brought you. Mel, you are more than I ever wanted. You are more than I knew I needed."

"Baby, I love you too! The first day I saw you I knew that there was something special about you. I knew that you were the one, and I was just hoping that you would feel the same way. You are my sunshine on a cloudy almost rainy day." We both giggled. Mel held my face. "I don't ever want to be without you. I don't care if you're old and fat with no teeth. I know I love you, and you are the only woman I ever felt loved me unconditionally." He gave me a kiss. "Now wipe your eyes, and let's go out here and entertain our family. For a minute there you scared me. I thought you were going to say no to a brotha's proposal."

"I may not be the smartest person in the world, but I am not a dummy. I know what I have in you." We walked out of the bathroom hand in hand.

I introduced Mel to the rest of the family and once introductions were over it was time to feast. "Okay let's eat everyone. I am hungry. How about you all?" Mel asked.

"Everyone follow us into the dining room. Mel really worked hard on some great dishes for you all. I can't pronounce them, but they are very delicious." I said as we all walked toward the dining room.

"I wished he woulda waited until I came ta propose ta ya, baby." Grandmother said as we walked into the dining room.

Everyone took a seat at the dining room table as Mel and I stood up. "Okay, this is always a special dinner to our family, and today it is even more special because we will have an addition!" I led the family in applause. "Mel has proposed to me, and as you know I said yes." I held up my left hand so that everyone could see my ring. "I'm sorry everyone didn't get to witness it, but just know that this is the happiest day in my life since I was born!" The room filled with laughter.

I continued. "I hope everyone loves this man

and welcomes him into our family as I love him. He's a great man." I turned to Mel and kissed him. Everyone cheered and applauded.

A great number of my family members were at our dinner: my grandmother Lenna May; my aunt Kissy May and her husband Deboize of 40 years; my uncle Bob and his wife Leana of 40 years and their daughter Canon; aunt Kissy May's daughter Mary and Mary's husband Paul of 20 years and their two kids Ashley and Manor; aunt Kissy May's son Todd and his wife Careen of 15 years and their son Isaac; and aunt Kissy May's youngest daughter Barbara who's expecting really soon, but none of us really know who the father of her child is. I suspect Aunt Kissy May is really ashamed of Barbara being pregnant out of wedlock, so everything is kept hush-hush. Knowing Aunt Kissy May, a shotgun wedding in somewhere in the plan.

My mother only had two siblings living. In my family we had strong and long marriages for the most part, so I always knew if I got married it would be to one man until death. My mother never remarried after the death of my father. I don't know why — she just didn't. My grandfather was deceased too, but he and my grandmother were married 60 years before he died. They married young.

"Okay everyone, Mel and I will go get dinner. I'm telling you, you all will enjoy Mel's cooking. He's a great cook." I raved. Mel and I walked toward the kitchen to get dinner.

"Ya got some chittlins, baby? Grandmother asked.

I turned around slightly. "No chitterlings Grandmother, but you are going to love what we do have."

"Grandmamma trust ya, baby. Bring it on out he'e. Grandmamma ready to eat, baby." Grandmother swayed from side to side. She spoke her mind at all times.

"Okay, grandmother." I was always patient with her.

The kitchen was opened to the dining room so we could still talk and interact with the family.

"Mama, all black people don't eat chittlins. That man looks like he takes care of his body. He ain't into eating no chittlins. We gettin' ready to have somethin' fancy. I can tell by looking at this house. Demisha found ha a rich man, honey. Demisha won't be eating no mo' chittlins, Mama. I knew that when we drove up in this neighborhood." I heard Aunt Kissy May say. "You saw that ring on her finger? Oh, mama, I forgot you can't see that far. You need to wear yo glasses. I don't know why you aint wearing yo glasses. Trying to stay all sexy and young with yo makeup. My daddy dead." Aunt Kissy May teased Grandmother.

"I don't like no glasses. Save 'em for at home.

Don't nobody wanna be looking at me with no glasses on my face." Grandmother retorted. Aunt Kissy May laughed.

"I'm like mama. I take care of my body too. I still was looking fa me some chittlins." Uncle Bob jumped in.

"Bob, what you doing to take care of yo body? How fast you can reach fa a remote don't count fa exercise." Aunt Kissy May chuckled. "You was breathing hard walking up the walkway jus nigh. I heard ya. I thought I was gonna haf-ta help Leana pick ya up off the ground. I sweated from the thought of it." She chuckled and waited on a comeback from Uncle Bob.

"I'm in shape. Shooood, I don't know what you talkin' bout. Tell 'em baby." He looked over at Leana a quick second. He didn't really want her to say anything. "My stomach use-ta hang over my belt. Now it hangs where ya can see my belt." He laughed at himself. Everyone else laughed too.

"Bob, you don't need no mo chittlins, man. You don ate so many chittlins ya look like a chittlin. Demisha could split that gut of yours right nigh, and we'll have chittlins fa every holiday. Some regular days too. You don had enough chittlins, man. You don't need-ta ask nobody else about chittlins. Sometimes ya gotta look at yoself in the mirror and recognize when it is time ta stop. Whenever ya got a beer gut and ya don't drink beer, it's time ta stop." Aunt Kissy May giggled.

"I don't get no complaints from my wife. She aint wen nowhere." Uncle Bob said.

"Where she gon go? She spent all ha life fattening you up. I wouldn't leave either. I wouldn't let nobody come take my pig and eat it after I spent my time fattening it up." Aunt Kissy May said. She was hilarious — funny without trying to be — her southern accent and how she stressed certain words. She loved teasing Uncle Bob, but no one was off limits to her. But she and Uncle Bob always had everyone laughing. My mother said Aunt Kissy May always teased Uncle Bob because when they were younger he teased Aunt Kissy May nonstop. So I guess now that they are older Aunt Kissy May is getting her justice. It was all in jest. My family always had a great time together. In fact, one would think they had sat down together and planned the show because their performance was always the life of the party.

"Do you need me to help you?" My mother asked me.

"They got it, Anna. Anna always wanna help, baby. That's yo' mama and my daughter. She been that way fa years." Grandmother said. She rocked back and forward and fidgeted with her hands. Not really talking to anyone, she continued. "She always helpn, helpn e'rybody. She was a little girl helpn e'rybody. That's my baby Anna."

Sometimes grandmother would think aloud.

She didn't dip snuff or chew tobacco, but she held her mouth like she did. She was a jazzy old lady. Grandmother wore thigh-high boots sometimes with her skirts. And she kept her hair golden blond or she wore a golden blond wig. She did not believe in gray hair. She had two gold crowns on her false teeth. She wore big diamond rings and fur coats. She even wore makeup. I think I got my spunk from her because my mother and I were total opposites sometimes.

"No, mama. You sit and rest. Mel and I have this. This is for you guys. We enjoyed doing this." I said.

My mother was so happy. She glowed. All she ever wanted was her baby to get married to someone special. She smiled from ear to ear, and she bragged about Mel as she sat at the table. Mel and I brought out the first couple of dishes, and then as we walked back into the kitchen my mother got up from her chair and followed us.

"Mother, I told you, you sit down this year." I said.

"I just want to tell ya something." She said.

"Okay, mama, if you insist you can take out the smaller dishes." I continued moving and getting things together to take out.

"No, stand still for one moment—the both of ya together." Mother said. Mel and I turned around to face her. "This is from the bottom of my heart. I am so happy for the two of ya. This is my baby right here, Mel, my only child. And I love her. I don't have to hear how good ya will be to her because I already know ya will. Ya just the kinda man that I asked God to bring into my baby's life." She put her hand on my face, and I kissed it. She reached for Mel's hand and held his hand. She continued to speak. "I don't care if ya don't give me any grandchildren. I am happy that ya two found each other. I can see the way ya love each other when ya look at each other. And it is beautiful. They don't make love like this anymore. I am extremely happy for the both of ya, and just as I am her mother, I am now yours. Keep God first because only God knows what the future brings. He can keep ya stronger than leather." She embraced us both. She even made Mel cry. Mother regained her composure. "Okay, I will wipe these tears and go back out here and sit with the rest of the family. Dinner not only smells good, it looks good!" She released us both and walked out of the kitchen.

"Did she just make me cry? She made me cry." Mel giggled. He was tough but very gentle at times. "Your mother is something special. I really love her." Mel wiped his eyes and grabbed another dish to take out to the table.

"Yes, she is. She is a praying woman. One day if I am lucky I will be just like her." I said.

After Mel and I brought out all the food, we sat down at the table with the rest of the family.

Mel said grace, and afterwards everyone talked and ate.

"Man, aint no chittlins, but this is good. Real good. Aint no pig nowhere on the table?" Uncle Bob asked a little perplexed and amazed simultaneously.

"No, Uncle Bob. I'm sorry." Mel answered.

"Bob, will you leave these kids alone 'bout some pig! Anyway, aint it against the law fa pig ta eat pig?" Aunt Kissy May said.

Loud laughter filled the room.

"There you go. You like you some pig too, Kissy." Uncle Bob retaliated.

"Yeah, but these are young people. They are tryin' ta keep their bodies in shape. They don't want ta take a thousand pills like we do. This here food is good. Don't need no pig, honey. I'm tryin' ta get off the pig myself." Aunt Kissy May said.

"You aint trying ta get off no pig! You been eatin' pig all yo life. She just gettin' all brand new 'cause she over here. My sister put pig in everything. She even put pig in ice cream. That's where I get it from." Uncle Bob chuckled.

"Aint nobody laughing but you. I know how to be classy. I don't haf-ta have a piece ah pig everywhere I go ta eat." Aunt Kissy May boasted.

"When was eating pig unclassy?" Uncle Bob

looked around humorously for someone to answer. "Shood, some of the classiest people I know eat pig." Uncle Bob chuckled. "I got a doctor friend. He love him some pig. Got enough money ta haf pig all kinda ways. Look at the people in Hawaii. They put a whole pig on the grill. I didn't even know pigs were runnin' round in Hawaii. Pig is nationwide. I don't know whatcha talkin' bout." He chuckled.

He had the men in tears. The women laughed too, but the men took it to another level.

"Leana, how you be married ta that man all yo life? All yo life!" Aunt Kissy May asked as she shook her head from side to side.

"Easy, she like pig too. And they don't get no classier than Leana. Shood, Leana eat pig eggrolls, pig sausages, pig fa breakfast, pig fa lunch, pig fa dinner, and she use-ta raise them when she was young." Uncle Bob said. Everyone laughed even Aunt Kissy May.

"You fa-got ta say and she sleep with one at night, you." Aunt Kissy May chuckled.

"Hey, whateva. We ain't shamed of our pig. You shamed of yo pig. Kissy high class now. She'll come down ta-morrow at breakfast, Mel, when she put that pig sausage in her mouth. I know my sista. Trust me. Been knowing ha all ha life. She haf ha moments where she gets high-dity. But when she open ha refrigerator ta-morrow, she comin' down to earth." Uncle Bob said. Aunt

Kissy May and her husband laughed so hard they all most spit out their food.

We all had a great time. It was a Thanksgiving we would all remember.

Once everyone left Mel and I sat in the living room exhausted holding each other. "Why didn't you tell me you were going to propose to me; I lost it!" I turned to face Mel.

"Then it wouldn't have been a surprise!" He tickled my side.

"Stop it! Mel, please!" I giggled. He stopped.

"I was surprised myself. But cooking with you in the kitchen made me realize just how special you are to me. Mike was with me when I bought the ring, and I told him I was going to ask you to marry me. He didn't know when because I didn't know when I was going to ask you. Everything just felt so good today. We were in the kitchen like husband and wife. I basically went with the flow because I want to feel the way I felt with you today for the rest of my life. I want to do you right in the sight of God because you deserve it. I know we didn't do everything right by God in the beginning, but it is never too late."

"You have been talking to my mother."

"She's been talking to me. Not about marriage but about God. Your mother rubs off on people, and that is a good thing. She doesn't even try to. She does it effortlessly. You can tell God is a big part of her life."

"God is her life. I never lived how she taught me, but I always remembered what she said."

"So when is the wedding?" He asked, and then he tried answering his own question. "Well, I was thinking more like Christmas. Christmas day! What do you think? No! What about tomorrow? The sooner the better! I want your stuff in here as soon as we can get it in here! I want these lips and hips next to me every night, right now." He smiled.

"Well, I was thinking more like Valentine's Day. I have always wanted a red and white wedding."

Mel raised his voice. "Please, baby that is too long! How does your family feel about you shacking? I can't wait until Valentine's Day to wake up to you every morning! Since you're back working it's hard for you to come all the way over here and spend the night with me when you have to be back on your side of town the very next morning. Sometimes I have to wait until the weekend to be with you. You mean to tell me that is enough for you?"

"Of course not. If it were, do you think I would be marrying you? Well, pick a day out of the air, and I will marry you then. But keep in mind that I want a wedding." Since he was upset about waiting three months, I thought it was best not to tell him I was referring to Valentine's Day in

1999 and not 1998. It took time to plan a wedding, and Mel didn't consider that. I thought we at least needed a year to plan. Valentine's Day in 1999 would have given us approximately fifteen months to get everything together.

"Did you not hear me? Christmas day it is then! We will move you in this month since it is only a few days until December."

"Baby, I can't just move." I giggled. "I have to give notice and pack my things. What is my mother going to say? You just said you want to do me right by God. I don't go to church, but even I know shacking isn't in his will."

"I'll hire some packers. They'll pack everything for you. We can pack your personal things ourselves. I'll pay to get you out of the lease."

"Mel, why can't I say no to you? I haven't met your mother yet. How will she feel knowing you have proposed to me, and she knew nothing about it?"

"You know how my mother and I are. Do you really think she didn't know I was going to propose to you? She knew. She was the first person I told."

"Oh, she knows."

"My mother kinda helped me pick out the ring even though she wasn't here. She told me the hottest new styles, and she sent me a couple of photos in the mail. She couldn't be here for Thanksgiving because she went out of town to visit my aunt. And I didn't know exactly when I was going to propose. As soon as she gets back she wants to meet you."

"I can't wait to meet the woman that had you. She sounds adorable over the phone."

"She is. She really is, and I am not just saying that because she is my mother. She'll do everything for me if I let her."

"So big wedding or small wedding?" I folded my legs Indian-style.

"Isn't this your thing? Well, I know I have about 150 people I would like to invite. I know my mother will probably have 50 outside of that." Mel didn't flinch.

"My goodness Mel, that's 200 people right there! I don't even think I know 200 hundred people that I would like to see at my wedding — maybe about 50 to 70." I paused as I thought about a few more people. "Well, maybe 100 including my family."

"Well, start making the list. Don't worry because I'm paying for everything!"

"You're serious?"

"Of course! My mother agreed to give me $20,000 as a gift once I told her I was going to ask you to marry me or should I say us as a gift. I didn't want to take it because we don't need it. But I know my mother, and it would be an insult to her if we didn't take it. So hopefully that can get your dress and take care of the reception. And I'll take care of the wedding and our honeymoon. Do you have any idea where you want to go for our honeymoon?"

I was still in disbelief. "I don't know! It's funny how when I never had a proposal I had all this stuff in my mind. Now I don't know. I'm just so happy! Maybe we can go to the Bahamas. Yeah, the Bahamas!"

"Well, I've never been there."

"Neither have I. I think we will love it. I have heard so much about it. I heard it's just as wonderful in the winter as it is in the summer. I'll ask this travel agent that I am familiar with and begin to make arrangements."

"I'm shocked you didn't say Hawaii."

"Why?"

"Because they have pigs in Hawaii. Pigs nationwiiiiiide." Mel said facetiously, imitating Uncle Bob.

"You are funny." I laughed.

"Not like ol' Uncle Bob. Aunt Kissy May was tagging him for a minute, but he didn't give up. He had a comeback. I love that chuckle he has. You got some good people — a down-to-earth family. I have never laughed so hard in my life. Are they always like that?"

"Yes, they are. It is a show that you do not have to pay to see. They love it. If Aunt Kissy May and Uncle Bob do not talk at each other, something is seriously wrong."

"Wow! I thought I was going to pee in my clothes, man. They need to take their act on the road."

"You are silly."

"Let's go to bed. I'm tired. It has been a long day and a hilarious night." Mel stood to his feet and pulled me up to mine.

"Mel, are you sure you want to marry me? You know I can be spoil and quite a baby when I want to be." I said humorously.

"Haven't I been spoiling you? All I want to do is spoil you. Now let's go to the bedroom so you can spoil me."

"Didn't you say you want to do me right by God?" I giggled.

"Yes. But it's a process. I am not there quite yet. But I put a ring on it, and I will marry you tomorrow if you let me. We can go to the justice of peace and have a wedding later for everyone else. I don't need a wedding."

"I want the wedding! Why don't we save the

milk until you buy the cow? Hey, the wedding date is right around the corner." I chuckled.

"Woman, don't you start." He said humorously.

"Seriously, Mel. Don't you think it would be wonderful if we waited until our wedding day?"

"What? Is that what you want to do, seriously?"

"I do, Mel. I really want God to bless us." I was sincere.

"He already blessed us with each other. But I know what you are saying. Why you had to spring this on a brotha? You give them the ring, and they want to get all high-dity and hold back the thing." He laughed as he referenced Uncle Bob again. "We will do whatever you want. I want God to bless us too."

"So I'll sleep in the other room."

"What! Dammmmn Demisha, I can't sleep next to those soft legs either! God, she is going too far. She is going toooooo far. Woman, I am not dealing with your high-dity ways. I read somewhere in the Bible a man put cover over his woman, and they were considered husband and wife. I have put cover over you several times. You are already my wife, woman."

"Stop playing, Mel."

"Babe, that is somewhere in the Bible. Adam and Eve didn't have a wedding, but they were husband and wife. Adam just woke up to a naked lady. It's in there! Naked lady just standing in front of him! That's why I know God is a man!" He chuckled. "In my heart and Spirit you are already my wife. I can't hold you at night, Demisha? Don't you think that is a little overboard?"

"You got the wedding date that you wanted, although I don't know how you are going to pull it off. Now give me this." I pleaded.

"Money will pull it off. Okay. I will do it for you." He walked ahead of me. "I hope the bedbugs bite the hell out of you!"

"No, you didn't. Funnn-ny." I giggled. "So you are going to leave me now?" I stopped as I watched Mel walk ahead of me.

"You are not sleeping with me. I don't need to wait on you." Mel smirked as he looked back at me. "You know where the other room is."

"All right, Mr. Funnyman. I am not laughing too hard."

"Adam just woke up to a naked woman in front of him. Hint, hint."

"Adam didn't leave Eve behind either."

"If I woke up to a buck-naked woman, I wouldn't have left her behind either." We laughed. "Pun intended." Mel added.

CHAPTER THREE

IT WAS MALISSA

By the first of December we had moved my things out of my apartment and into Mel's house. Mel hired a moving crew.

I stood in my empty apartment saying my last goodbyes to it when I got emotional. Stacy walked in. "Hey girl, what are you doing?" She asked.

I sighed. "I'm just saying goodbye to this place, girl." I wiped the tears from my eyes and then I continued. "You know this is where I spent most of my single life — all the ups and downs. I won't miss the lifestyle, but I will miss my place. You know how it is."

"Yes, I do. I am going to miss youuuu! You know I love you. You have been the best neighbor a person could ever have. I am coming to see you, and you better not forget that I am here." Stacy's emotions took over. She reached over and hugged me.

"You know I will never forget you, Stacy. How can I? You have been a mother, a sister, a friend, and a counselor to me. When you cooked for your family you cooked for me. I will never forget you, girl. Give these keys to Mr. Anderson for me, and I love you. Tell Cameron I said goodbye."

"Okay, I will. But my mother said don't say goodbye. Say I will see you later."

"I will see you later, Stacy."

We walked out of the front door. Stacy walked me out to my car. "Girl, you know I'm going to miss you — miss cooking dinners for you. But I must say that I am so happy for you. You make sure I get my invitation."

"You should get it soon."

"I thought you wanted a Valentine's Day wedding."

"You know too much about me. He didn't want to waste too much time. He's been talking to my mother."

"Oh, okay. That says a mouthful."

"Yes, it does."

"Mike has to find him a new club partner now." She giggled.

"Yes, he does."

"But he will probably get married soon after you. Now that he knows he cannot have you. Mike always loved you."

"You think so?"

"I know so."

"He is really happy for me. He and Mel are great friends. He knew Mel was going to propose to me before I knew."

"What! He loves you enough to let you go and see you happy. He might as well. Can't do nothin' bout it anyway."

"Girl, do you ever hold inside what is in that brain of yours?" I giggled.

"Girl, no! Whatever comes up comes out."

"I know. That is what I am going to miss. I am going to miss you barging in my place like it is an extension of yours."

"Yeah, I hope I get a good neighbor. I don't need a fuddy-duddy living next door to me. It will not work, and I will have to send Poo over there to doo-doo on their porch."

"Girl, you are a mess!" I giggled. "Let me get out of here."

"Okay. See you later, Demisha. Don't forget where I live." Stacy smiled.

"I won't." I pulled off and waved goodbye. I cried as I drove away. I think I cried so much because I really had no faith that I would get married and leave my bachelorette pad. So leaving my place was surreal to me. I talked a good game, but truth is I talked a good game to keep from crying. Some days I succumbed to the thought of being an old maid.

As I drove my cell phone rang. "Hello." I answered it.

"Hey Baby-girl." It was Mike.

"Hey Mike. I just left my old place. It was hard, man. It was hard."

"Oh yeah." He sighed.

"What's wrong, dude?" I asked because Mike didn't sound right. He sounded rather dry. "What is it?"

"Ya know I am so happy for ya. Ya know I always wanted the best for ya."

Immediately I thought about Stacy and our recent conversation. "Mike, why are you telling me this? You know I know that you love me, and I know that you are happy for me. You're not sounding right. What is really going on?"

"Can ya come over here? I need ya right now."

It worried me that Mike didn't sound like himself. I knew Mike well, and I knew when there was something wrong with him, which was hardly ever. Mike was a very unusually happy person even when things didn't seem to go his way. So I knew that if he said he needed to see me, he really felt low.

"Let me call Mel at the store to let him know I won't be home right away, and I'm on my way." I was concerned about Mike.

"Okay, I'll see ya." Mike said. Something had stolen the life from him. I hoped it was not what Stacy and I discussed. I didn't want to hear my best friend tell me he loved me. I didn't want to break his heart again. I thought that Mike and I were over this. I tried to think about how to let him down easy. He is my best man — the person that is going to be right by my side in my wedding. What is Mel going to think when I tell him Mike is still in love with me? Should I tell Mel?

When I pulled up in Mike's driveway I didn't call him on my cell phone like I would usually do to let him know I was there. I just jumped right out of the car and rang the doorbell. I rang the doorbell a couple of times, and then I called his name.

"Mike!" I yelled. "Mike!"

He finally came to the door. His eyes were red as fire. He looked as if he had been crying. I stepped inside. "Mike, what is wrong? Tell me! I have plenty of time. I was able to reach Mel, so he knows that I'm going to be late. Talk to me. What's up?" I said with a weird nervous feeling taking over my body. Mike and I walked over to his kitchen table and sat down.

"I'm not doing well, Demisha. I'm not." Mike said as he held his head down and shook it from side to side.

Oh Lord, here we go. Let me play dumb. "What's wrong? Some woman? No, that can't be it. You didn't tell me that you were serious with anyone. What is it, Mike? I don't like seeing you this way."

"Demisha, I have been feeling so weak lately, and I have been coughing up blood."

Good grief, it's worse than I thought. What would Stacy tell me to say? "Mike, you never told me anything about that. How long has this been going on?"

"Awhile now. I didn't think it was anything to worry about."

"Well Mike, what is it?" I put my hand on his

shoulder and caressed him. I saw a tear leave his eye. I wasn't prepared for this. He was still in love with me just like Stacy said.

"Demisha, I don't want to tell ya." He cried.

By this time I was perplexed and scared simultaneously. Mike was a very hard man. He didn't cry at the drop of a dime, so I didn't know what to think. "Mike, why are you crying? Tell me what it is? You know I don't like seeing you this way. You're too strong for this."

"I have—" He didn't finish his sentence.

"You have what, Mike? What is it? I'm your best friend, and I am here through everything! Tell me."

"Demisha, I have AIDS. I am dying! I'm dying!" Mike cried harder, and he reached over and hugged me tightly.

Wait a minute. I didn't hear what I thought I was going to hear. My mouth was wide open and I couldn't close it. I couldn't hold Mike because his news had paralyzed me. It wasn't very long before my brain replayed what he said, and I broke down. We held each other for a moment without letting go. After a few minutes he sat up straight, and he wiped my tears away.

"I don't believe it." I dropped my head.

"Demisha, it's true. I took the test before Thanksgiving. I am dying. I have known that I was dying for a few days now, but I was in denial. Ya can't be in denial too."

"Why didn't you call me sooner?"

"I knew ya were moving, and I am so happy for ya, Demisha. I-am-very-happy–for-ya. Why would I burden ya with this? I didn't want to tell ya now, but I had to for ya sake."

"Where or who did you get it from? Do you know?"

"I had a chance to call around to the three women I had unprotected sex with. Well, we both know Demisha that ya one of them, my daughter's mother, and the other one was —" He dropped his head without finishing his sentence again.

"Was who, Mike?"

"It was Malissa. Malissa is the one who gave it to me. My daughter's mother was before Malissa, and she doesn't have it. She told me she takes an HIV test every three months because she had some blood spilled on her in the hospital about two years ago."

"The girlfriend you had before me?"

Mike dropped his head again. "Yes Demisha. Baby-girl, I am so sorry." He raised his head. "I never meant to hurt ya!"

My brain was still stuck on Mike being in love with me, so it took me a minute to realize what

Mike was intimating. "I'm all right. I haven't been feeling weak at all. I haven't! Besides, look at how many years ago it's been! No! No! Not me!"

"Please Demisha, know that I am sorry. All I am saying is get a test done. Ya know that I would never hurt ya purposely."

"Mike, stop saying that. I don't believe it! At first it was you, and now it might be me too? Damn Mike! If this is a joke, it sure isn't funny."

"No, no, not you. I just want ya to get a test. It's a chance ya might not have it! There is a chance!" Mike gained his strength to console me.

"How far are you? What's wrong with you? Why are you vomiting blood?"

"Well, I have to get more tests done. Ya have to get the first test done, but I have full-blown AIDS. I do know that for sure — blood cells."

"I'm so scared for you, Mike. I'm scared, Mike! Oh God, I don't know what to say. So you say it was Malissa. How do you know? Do you know for sure?"

"Well, I called Malissa's mother, and Malissa died three years ago. When I asked her mother what she died of, she was surprised that I didn't know. She said Malissa should have contacted me before she got real sick."

"Maybe she couldn't find you."

"I don't know why the hell not. I found her when I found out I had this shit!"

"So basically you have been infected all this time — all this time. Had you ever taken a test before this?"

"Yes, but the last time was right before I met Malissa, about seven years or so ago. Hell, I don't know. What about you, when was ya last one?"

"I took one about four years ago. I was good then, but after this news I don't know. I never had unprotected sex like that. I only have unprotected sex in a committed relationship, and you know I haven't had many of those. You were really the only person I ever committed to other than Mel. Mel and I stop having sex until the wedding, but even when we did, we used condoms."

"I only have unprotected sex in committed relationships too. But maybe before I committed to taking the condom off with Malissa, I should have gone with her and we both got tested. Damn!" Mike got frustrated.

"It is seven o'clock, Mike. I have to go. I have got to talk to Mel. Are you going to be okay?"

"Yes, I am. Are ya going to be okay?"

"Of course I will. I'm worried about you." I leaned over and pecked Mike's lips. "Don't worry because we are going to get through this like we do everything else. I heard people live a long time with this disease."

"Yeah right." Mike said hopelessly. "Let me walk you to your car."

"Mike, we will make it through this. We will. You have to stay strong and positive. I am getting ready to embark on a new chapter in my life. I'm getting married, so I have to stay positive."

I watched Mike as I pulled away in my car. Did he really tell me he had AIDS or was I dreaming? I thought telling me he loved me romantically would be bad, but telling me he had AIDS was worse. My head was so cluttered after I left Mike. What in the world went wrong here? Everything was going so well. Maybe I don't have it, but I have to deal with watching my best friend die. Mike has AIDS. What happened to HIV? I have got to be there for him whether I have it or not.

I could tell there was something wrong with Mike, but I was caught up in my own happiness. Mike's skin textured had changed. His silky smooth skin had become blotchy and bumpy. I mentioned it to Mel, but I thought no more about it. Maybe it was something he was eating or stressing over. I never thought it was AIDS. How will I tell Mel? Can I tell Mel? I have moved all of my stuff out of my place and turned in the keys to my apartment. Where will I go now? I'll go to my mother's, but it will worry her. I'll have to see her worry day in and day out. Okay, first I have to tell Mel the situation. I can be woman enough and tell him whether he hates me or not. My mother

raised me to be a woman about things. I can tell
him.

"Hey lady, watch where you are going!"
Some man yelled as I swerved into his lane a little.

I swerved back into my lane. "Oh, I am
sorry!" I shouted.

How could God let this happen to me? My
fairy tale was ending fast.

CHAPTER FOUR

HE LEFT ME

As I pulled into the driveway Mel came out of the garage waiting on me to pull the car in. He looked so handsome, as gorgeous as the first night I met him. I pulled the car into the garage. Mel followed behind me.

He opened my door. "You're home, love. When you called me and said you were going to be late I had no idea it would be this late. Is something wrong? You don't look too right."

"Let's go inside." I said.

We entered the house from the side door inside of the garage. "Something is wrong." Mel surmised.

"Mel, I'm not all right." I looked at the boxes that had come from my apartment that were labeled kitchen. My eyes teared up.

"Baby, what's wrong? I'm here for you." He assured me.

"Mel, you mean so much to me. I love you with all my heart. You make me feel so good inside and out. I felt the love of God when you came into my life and covered me with your love. And it all happened so fast. I was single for almost all my life, and then you walked right into my life and changed everything. Everything! I still can't fathom it all."

"I don't have to know what it is right now. I don't want to know — how about that. We can wait until later, baby." He said gently. He didn't want to end the love story.

"No, it wouldn't be fair to you. I want you to sit down. Come on let's sit down." We walked into the living room and took a seat on the sofa.

"You want some music on? I know music makes you feel better."

"No Mel, this is serious. There is no way I can relax telling you this. Look at me." I kissed his lips as I looked into his beautiful brown eyes because I knew that what I was about to say would make them blue. When Mike told it to me, it made my brown eyes blue.

"Mel, when I called and told you that I would be late it was because Mike needed me. He called me on my cell phone. He was sad and hurt about something."

"Okay, what is it?"

"Mel, Mike has AIDS. Mike has AIDS. And I am very hurt for him because he is dying Mel, and he knows it! He hid his symptoms from me because he didn't want to worry me, but he had a test done. He has the disease. The person that infected him is dead now. She died a few years ago. She was —"

Mel interrupted me. "Okay, slow down. You have said too much too fast. Mike has AIDS. Okay, how is he doing?"

"Not so well."

"Is it HIV or AIDS because a lot of people confuse the two?"

"It's AIDS. At least that is what he told me. Hell, I don't know. It blew my mind. Here I am the happiest I have ever been, and then my best friend calls me over to his place to tell me he has AIDS. I am sick to my stomach right now!"

"Wow! Breathe. Okay, I feel bad for my brotha. But it is not a death sentence. He can turn this thing around. He has us."

"That is not all."

"Okay."

"He and I had unprotected sex after we were together for eight months, so for a year and like four months of our relationship we had unprotected sex! We were committed! Committed people have unprotected sex! Right?"

Mel dropped his head. "We haven't." That's all he said and got up and walked upstairs. It was like a scene from a movie. I didn't try to stop him.

I took one of the pillows off the sofa and placed it under my knees. And I just cried out to God. I prayed for Mike, and I prayed for Mel and me. I must have prayed for an hour. I didn't know I could pray that long. I guess when you really need God you can do anything to reach God. I fell asleep on the sofa.

I awoke from a soft kiss on my lips and a touch on my hand. I opened my eyes, and it was Mel. He had on the same clothes. He was fully dressed.

"It is late, baby. You've been asleep here for hours." Mel said.

"It's morning? What time is it?"

"It's after midnight."

I sat up on the sofa rubbing my eyes. "I have to be at work in the morning."

"No, I don't want you to work in the morning. We will get your test done, together. I'll get tested too. We will make it a couple's thing."

"Mel, you shouldn't have it. We haven't had unprotected sex. At least I hope you don't think you have it."

"I am not worried about having it. We don't even know if you have it. Don't claim it. I just want to be right by your side supporting you. It will be better if we do it together. How is your mother coming along with planning the wedding?"

My eyes got bigger. He shocked me because he still wanted to marry me. "You, you, you still want to marry me?" I stuttered.

"I love you, and love doesn't die that easy — at least not for me. My love could never die for you because of words." He squeezed me.

Mel touched my heart. God answered my prayers. I was full of joy because I didn't want to lose Mel. I had tasted God's goodness, and I wouldn't know how to turn back. I knew Mel was a part of God's plan for me.

I lifted my head from his chest. I wanted to make sure I understood what he said. "What if I have it? What then?"

"Well, you will still have me, if you'll have me. I am just as anxious for you to be my wife now as I was before you told me this. Come on, let's get us some sleep. And you can call in sick later. I turned down your covers on your bed."

Later that morning Mel and I went to a private doctor. We were both counseled and tested for HIV. It was extremely difficult walking out of the doctor's office knowing that there was a great possibility that I had contracted AIDS. We had to wait three days for the results. The doctor said he would give us a call as soon as the results were ready. Out of everything, waiting was the hardest part. Mel felt that it would be best for us not to tell anyone what was going on until we had the results. I agreed, so we didn't tell anyone.

I went to work as usual. As I taught my students I didn't think much about the results of the HIV test. But when I had a moment alone I would sometimes drift off and think about the test results.

At the end of our work days, Mel and I would meet up at Mike's house and spend time with him. Mike's house was so dark. He had clothes everywhere, which was very unlike him. Mike was always very clean before being diagnosed with AIDS. He was so clean that I suspected he had a cleaning disorder but had not been diagnosed with it. So when Mel and I visited Mike we would clean up, open the blinds, and make sure he ate something. While there, we were able to see the effects of his sickness. He coughed uncontrollably and a few times he coughed up blood. It was scary for me because every time I looked at Mike I saw myself.

He didn't tell his parents or his daughter about his illness. His daughter's mother knew, but she wanted Mike to tell their daughter about his condition.

One evening Mel and I really had a long talk with Mike. "Mike, you can't live like this, baby. I know it's hard. But you have to get a grip because regardless of what, you can live a very long time the doctors say. The more you become depressed the faster your life will fade. You have to tell your family. They can help you through this too." I said. I sat beside him on the sofa, and Mel sat in front of us in a chair.

"Are ya still waiting on ya test results? Do ya know the results yet?" Mike asked desperately looking at me. He acted as if he didn't hear a word I said.

"No, I'll know for sure tomorrow. It will be the third day. We will tomorrow, tell him Mel." I tried to comfort Mike.

"Yes, we will." Mel said. Mel didn't like seeing Mike so despondent. He and Mike had become great friends, and Mike seemed to be falling apart all of a sudden. It just didn't seem right.

"I'm so sorry Mel to put ya through this. I know how much ya love Demisha. I know how much she loves ya. Ya really good for her. All I want is for Baby-girl to be happy, and you make her happy." Mike said as he reached for my hand and smiled at Mel. Mike was so worried about me that he forgot about himself. Any other time I would be flattered, but there was nothing flattering about seeing my friend deteriorate in front of my eyes.

"You never meant to intentionally put her at risk. You guys had a relationship, and you made adult decisions. So I don't blame you for anything. I love Demisha and nothing can stop that. Demisha loves you as her friend, and whatever she loves I love. Even before I knew just how cool you are, I liked you because she loved you. You can do better, man. You have got to have the will to live. Don't give up. The way you are living is like you are giving up. And I don't like to see you give up!" Mel got emotional.

"It seemed like yesterday I was so healthy — so strong. And in a matter of days I find myself coughing up my insides, feelin' cold all the time, and gettin' very weak. I never even thought it was this serious. I'm losing it, man! I'm losing it." Mike said.

We encouraged Mike and at the same time encouraged ourselves because Mike's house was gloomy. When Mike was happy and full of life, his house was happy. But now that he was sick, it felt as if something dark was hovering over his house. It was weird.

I hated seeing Mike go through what he was

going through, and God knew I didn't want to go through it. I prayed the entire time Mel and I waited for our results.

On the day the results were ready, I was a nervous wreck in school. Although I taught young students, they recognized my reckless behavior. I had to get one of the assistants to sit in my class for half an hour pass my lunch. I tried to unscramble my nerves. When I returned from lunch I had only an hour left before school would be dismissed. I kept my eyes on the clock the entire time. It didn't take long for the hour to pass. And as soon as the parents picked up all of the students, I left school.

I waited patiently for Mel to come home from work. He arrived home earlier than usual because he knew we had to get the results of the tests. As soon as Mel pulled into the driveway I walked out to his truck. We took his truck.

"Are you nervous, baby? Everything is going to be okay. Don't worry." Mel said trying to comfort me as I hopped in the truck. I wanted Mel to be quiet the rest of the way, but he didn't. Once I was in the truck he kept talking. "We will get married, take our honeymoon, and come back and have some kids." He chuckled. I smiled briefly. I didn't want to smile too long because I thought it would encourage him to continue talking. The brief smile didn't work. Mel kept right on talking. "See, I knew I could get you to smile. Your smile is so beautiful. That's why I fell in love with you.

Your smile told me you were going to be the woman of my life. And that spicy attitude you came with turned me on! I love you all the way down to your crooked baby-toes." Mel tried to keep the mood light. It worked a little because I laughed.

When we arrived at the doctor's office, my palms were sweaty. I felt paralyzed in my seat.

Mel cut the truck off. "Okay baby we are here. Are you okay?"

"I'm okay. I want to know the results — that's all." My voice trembled, but I still didn't move.

"Well baby, you have to get out of the truck and go into the office to do that. It's going to be okay. You have me, and I have you."

Mel and I walked arm and arm into the doctor's office. We walked into the waiting area and took a seat. "I'm going to go up and check us in." Mel said. He walked to the front desk to check us in.

The doctor was expecting us. I sat nervously in the waiting area, but I was relieved that the waiting area was not crowded. There were only two other people.

"Baby, I've been thinking, if I have the virus maybe we shouldn't get married. I mean, you deserve better than what I would be able to give you. You deserve someone who expects to live longer not someone who knows they are going to die. Someone who can give you kids." I whispered.

"Please, what are you saying? The best days of my life have been with you. Why shouldn't you be my wife? I love you. We don't have to have kids! Don't talk like this. Let's wait on the doctor. You playing a hand that hasn't been dealt yet." He paused and then he continued. "We all have to die one day. I'm not living forever either. I remember what you said about making my brown eyes blue the day you told me that you needed to get tested. Do you remember?"

"Yes, I remember."

"Well, don't make your beautiful, beautiful brown eyes blue worrying about this test. I love you. You're going to be my wife, and we are going to be happy. Stop giving up on me so soon." Mel kissed me.

"Ms. Coleman and Mr. Underwood." The nurse called us to the front desk as she held our charts in her hand. We walked to the desk holding hands. "Now I know that you guys are together. Would you like to be in the same room or separate rooms?" The nurse asked us.

"We want to be together, if that is okay with the doctor." Mel said.

"Oh that's fine. Come through the side door and follow me." When we walked through the side door she led us to a room.

"Okay you can take this room here, and the doctor will be with you in a moment." The nurse left the room and closed the door. The room was cold and bright. There were only two chairs and an examining bed in the room. Mel stood up as he leaned against the examining bed, and I sat in one of the chairs. It was quiet. We could hear the other patients a little in the other rooms. Finally, the door to our room opened and the doctor walked in. I took a deep breath.

"How are you guys doing today?" The doctor asked not really giving either of us eye contact.

"We are fine doctor." Mel said. I couldn't say a word. I smiled I guess. If I didn't, I purposed in my mind to smile.

"Because you two are in here together I know that it is okay to share your results. Let me start by saying there are many treatments for the virus that have helped many people live long happy lives. So a positive status is never a death sentence." What the hell did he say that for? I knew for sure one of us, if not both, had the virus. Tears just trickled down my face uncontrollably. Mel was quiet. He had lost his cool. He stiffened up, and his eyes were stuck in a stare. "Mr. Underwood, we will start with you first. Your results are negative. You do not have the HIV virus, but it's always good to get a test every year. In certain circumstances, I recommend three to six months."

Mel let out a sigh of relief, and then he looked

over at me and reached for my hand. He held it tight as the doctor picked up my chart.

The doctor continued. "Ms. Coleman, I am very sorry." I didn't hear anything else after that.

"No, no!" I stood to my feet and yelled. Mel grabbed me and held me tight.

"I am so sorry, Mr. Underwood. I am going to leave you two alone and before you go we can talk because there are ways she can beat this thing. There is no cure, but this is not a death sentence. People live for years with this virus. I'll come back."

"So doctor, she has the virus? Is that what you are saying?" Mel asked. I guess Mel was in denial because I understood loud and clear what the doctor said. Was my screaming not a clue? I guess Mel wanted to hear him say it another way.

"Yes. I am very sorry. Although I am a doctor, I hate being the bearer of bad news. I'll leave and give you two a little time. Then we can talk about things she can do to fight this. It is going to be okay."

"Okay." Mel responded as he held on to me and rocked me like a baby. I was devastated and there was nowhere for me to run or hide. What I feared came to pass.

The drive home was somber. Mel was very quiet and so was I. He drove the car with his left hand and held my hand with his right. It was all clear to me. I knew that I would never have any kids. And I would die leaving Mel alone — if he stayed with me. He said he would, but now it was real. If he decided to leave, I wasn't going to blame him. I would be hurt, but I would understand. What will my mother do without me? How can I tell her I am HIV positive?

Mel interrupted my thinking. "Baby, we are home. Come on. Wait, I'll come around and help you out." Mel helped me out of the truck. He held me close to him as we walked up to the house. The test results crippled me.

Mel cooked dinner after walking me to my room to rest. He brought dinner to my room. Mel didn't say much to me at all. He didn't try to make me laugh anymore because there was nothing funny. I presumed he was changing his mind about marrying me, and I didn't blame him. If we could end it being good friends, that would suffice.

I took a shower after dinner, and Mel stayed downstairs. After I showered I went downstairs to tell Mel goodnight. He sat on the sofa in front of the lit fireplace listening to Anita Baker. The lights were dimmed. "Baby, I'm getting ready to go to bed." I said.

"Oh, you're out of the shower. No, I want you to stay right here with me and dance with me. I want to hold you close to me. Do you hear what's playing? It's your favorite song. Come on and dance with me."

"Mel, I don't feel like dancing."

"Come on, baby, let's dance." Mel took hold of me. We danced as the music played and Mel sang along with the music. "I'm caught up in the rapture of love, baby."

Dancing did make me feel better. For a brief moment I forgot all my troubles.

****

That weekend Mel and I went over to my mother's house to tell her the news. I was so afraid to tell her. Now I could comprehend Mike's hesitance about telling his family his status. When we got to my mother's house she was elated to see us.

"Hey! I am so happy to see ya guys." Mother said as she opened her arms to hug and kiss us. "Come on in, come on in! Mama cooked today. My mind told me to cook because someone would be coming to eat. It's my favorite two people at that." She walked ahead of us through the house.

"What did you cook, Mother?" Mel asked.

"I cooked some collard greens, smoke neck bones, cornbread, and homemade macaroni and cheese! Oh, and I made some sweet tea with lemons too."

"You did it up, and I'm going to do it in! I like a little sweet tea sometimes." Mel giggled and rubbed his hands together. "May I go in the kitchen and get myself a lil somethin'?"

"Sure, baby. I will come and fix ya something." Mother enjoyed catering to people.

"No, mother. Is it okay if Mel serves himself so that we can talk?" I asked.

"Oh. Well, Mel, ya know where everything is. Go on in and feed yourself." Mother told Mel.

"Okay." Mel walked into the kitchen while mother and I stayed in the living room.

"Anything wrong, baby? Ya don't want nothing to eat? Ya know I just about have everything ready for the wedding. All the invitations were sent out when I got Mel's guest list, and I just need ya to try on ya dress and Mike and Mel to try on their tuxedos. Everything will be fine, so don't ya worry yourself. Mama has everything under control. Have ya met Mel's mother yet? I am looking forward to meeting her." Mother talked so fast, and she didn't take a breath until she was finished.

"No, mother, but she will be in town tomorrow."

"That's great, maybe she can go to church with me."

"Mother, slow down please. I have something to tell you, and it is not about the wedding or Mel's mother." I grabbed hold of both of her hands.

"What's wrong, child? Tell me what's wrong." A concerned look took over her face.

"Mother, there is no easy way to tell you this. I tried to think of many ways, but there is no easy way."

"What? You and Mel okay?"

"Mother. Mel, could you please come in here?" Mel walked into the living room from the kitchen, and he sat near me.

"Mother, I am dying." I said. Mother let out a loud gasp.

"She is not dying! Baby, don't scare mother like that. Tell her in a better way." Mel said perturbed by my bluntness.

"There is no better way." I cried.

"There is! Mother, Demisha is not dying. She has HIV."

"Same thing." I said.

"Stop it, Demisha. Just stop it!" Mel said.

"Oh, no! No, not my baby! Not my baby!" My mother jumped to her feet, and I jumped up with her. She cried and started shaking. I knew she was going to take it hard, but she was hysterical. She cried and screamed like I was already dead. I forgot about me and tried hard to console her.

"Mother, I am not going to die! I am sorry! I shouldn't have said it like that! Calm down, mama." It scared me to see my mother shaking uncontrollably.

"Sit her down! Let me get her something to drink. Damn it, Demisha!" Mel ran into the kitchen to get mother something to drink.

"I said I was sorry! Mother, please calm down."

It took an hour to calm my mother down. And after we calmed her down, it took another thirty minutes to explain to her how I contracted the virus. She had knowledge about HIV. In fact, she saw many cases in her days of being a nurse. Maybe that is why she took the news so hard. She saw people die horrible deaths from HIV/AIDS. We didn't have to educate her about the disease. She educated us once she could talk and think straight. She was not upset with Mike. She wanted to take time out to visit him after I told her about his depression.

We arrived at my mother's house about two o'clock that day, and we didn't leave for home until about eleven o'clock that night. I didn't have what it took to tell everyone in my family that I had HIV, so my mother said that she would handle it later. It surprised her to hear that the wedding plans were still on. She kissed Mel repeatedly on each cheek when he told her that we were still getting married. And again she acknowledged how blessed she was to have such a great son-in-law. But she was very hurt and afraid for me. I believed if she could have traded places with me, she would have.

When Mel and I got home Mike was on the answering machine several times. He knew we were supposed to get the results. I hesitantly gave him a call. I hated sharing bad news all day.

"Hello." Mike answered his phone.

"Hey, Mike. How are you doing?" I asked. I tried to conceal any unhappiness, so I turned up my energy.

"I'm fine. How about you? How are ya doing?" Mike asked.

"Oh, I am great. Mel and I just left mother's house. She cooked a big dinner, and we ate until we couldn't eat any more. I'm a little tired." I yawned. "But I got your messages, and I wanted to call you back."

"How was it?" Mike asked.

"Oh, it was good. Mel is tired too. We stayed over mother's house a long time." I yawned again hoping that Mike would let me get off the phone.

"Ya know what I'm talking about, Demisha. How were ya test results? Tell me the truth."

I sighed. I didn't want to tell him, but I knew I had to level with him. I remained upbeat. "I tested positive for HIV. Hey, Mel didn't. And he is still going to marry me, Mike! The doctor said I can really live a long time with it, so don't blame yourself. You can live a long time too, Mike. We are going to fight!" I tried to avoid staying on the negative.

"Oh, Demisha! I'm so sorry I did this to ya! Demisha, I love ya. I would never hurt ya purposely. Never!" Emotions took over Mike. It went exactly where I tried to keep it from going. I struck out with my mother, and I struck out with Mike. I couldn't win.

"Mike, I know you would never intentionally hurt me. You don't have to convince me. No one blames you. You are a victim like me. And although we are victims, we are adults. We made the decision to have unprotected sex. So please don't blame yourself! I am going to fight. You are going to fight! We are going to be all right. You'll see. We are going to grow old just like we planned." I hoped we could end our conversation so that I could go to sleep. We could deal with it in the morning. Being the bearer of bad news all day was depleting.

"It's my fault though, Demisha. Ya just so forgiving. Ya just so sweet although ya try to be so hard. But ya could never fool me. I always knew that ya were a lion with a big heart. I love ya, Demisha." Mike said softly.

I dropped my head a little as I held the phone. I was sad because I didn't want Mike to blame himself, and I knew he did. Mike loved me so much that I knew I was the last person he ever wanted to hurt. "Mike, are you going to be okay?"

"Of course I am. Everything will be better by tomorrow. It will. I am just sorry that I ruined ya life. I love ya so much. I wanted ya to be my wife. But when I saw that it wasn't what ya wanted, I just wanted ya to be happy. I remained ya friend because I had to have ya in my life somehow. I was so happy when you found Mel. I'm so sorry." I heard the phone click. He hung up the phone. I tried to call him back, but I kept getting a busy signal. I couldn't rest. I knew he was probably crying his eyes out.

"I did it again." I said to Mel as I continued to dial Mike's number.

"You did what?" Mel asked.

"I depressed Mike with my test results. I was gingerly this time. But the news depressed him."

"You're his best friend. If the news didn't make him sad I would be shocked. Stop talking about it. It takes too much energy from you."

"Mel, we have got to go over to Mike's. Something is wrong! I can't get him back. Now, the phone is busy. He was very somber about my results. He blamed himself. He just didn't sound right, Mel. He didn't sound right."

"Maybe he's okay. Everybody needs some sleep. It has been a long day. We will deal with everything tomorrow."

"No, Mel. Something isn't right — trust me. I know that it's late, but I know Mike well. And something isn't right. He didn't even say bye. He just hung up."

"Well, I'm happy I didn't get my clothes off. Let's go because I know you will not be able to sleep if we don't." Mel grabbed the keys to his truck.

It took us almost twenty minutes to get to Mike's house. When we pulled up in his driveway, there were no lights on in his house that pierced the outside. Even the garage lights were off. At night his garage lights automatically came on. He must have disconnected them I thought.

I jumped out of the truck before Mel could turn it off. "Mike, Mike!" I yelled as I ran up to his house.

When I got to the door, I tried to beat the door down. Mel ran up to the door behind me. "Baby, hold on. Calm down before you wake his neighbors! You ring the doorbell, and I will go 'round back and see if I can get him to open up." Mel crept around back.

"Okay." I rang the doorbell, knocked on the door, and yelled his name simultaneously. Mike never came to the door. I was positive that something was wrong because I knew that he was not a heavy sleeper, and we had just talked thirty minutes earlier. A neighbor walked across the grass. I assumed she heard me yelling.

"Hey, I have called the police."

"Why? I'm his friend! That is my fiancé that went around back!"

"No, no, not on you. I have seen you all before. I heard two gunshots earlier, and I walked outside and didn't see anything." The neighbor said as she stood holding her robe together.

"Gunshots? Mike didn't own a gun. They didn't come from Mike's house. Gunshots!" I said.

"Well, I heard them. They startled me. We don't hear that in this neighborhood, so I am sure that is what I heard." She said.

I politely turned back to Mike's door ignoring the neighbor. Mike had told me how a lot of his neighbors were high-strung and nosy. She probably heard something fall but surely not gunshots. "Mike! Mike!" I yelled.

The door opened, but it was Mel. "Oh Mel you got in!" Relief removed the tension from my body. "Where is Mike? Is he okay, Mel? He has the freakiest neighbors. Why didn't he answer? Damn neighbor scaring me to death!"

Mel eyes didn't look right and his face was ironed stiff. "Baby, I think Mike is gone!"

"He can't be gone his stuff is still here. We just talked."

"Not like that, baby. I think he killed himself." Mel said as he grabbed hold of me.

"You sound like that crazy neighbor of his! Mike! Mel, let me go inside! He can't be gone. We were just talking on the phone! We were just talking! Miiiiiiiikkkke!" I yelled at the top of my lungs.

Mel restrained me from going pass the foyer. "No, baby, you don't need to go in there! I know it hurts. It will hurt more if you see him that way!" I went limp in Mel's arms.

Mike ended his life with one gunshot to his head, and the other gunshot that the neighbor said she heard was the result of the gun falling to the floor. Mike was buried December 15, 1997. He left behind his mother, a stepfather, two sisters, his daughter, and me.

Mike had a very private funeral with less than 60 people in attendance. Saying goodbye to Mike was very difficult. His death hurt me so bad that I postponed my wedding for February 14th. I wanted to push it off longer, but Mel didn't think we should wait too long since we were already living together.

To my surprise, Mike appointed me as executor of his estate. He also left me a $1,000,000 life insurance policy, but because he committed suicide I only received half of that amount. He had a separate policy with his daughter and parents as the beneficiaries. I sold all of his

property and divided the money among his
family.

CHAPTER FIVE

TRYING TO GO ON

After Mike's funeral, Demisha took a holiday hiatus. She rested, and when she wasn't resting she went to see a psychiatrist — one of Mel's friends. Mel never told the psychiatrist what Demisha had gone through. He left that to Demisha.

The psychiatrist name was Donna. Demisha saw her in the beginning five days a week. She gave Demisha someone to talk to who was new to her life. Donna was only four years older than Demisha. She was not the typical psychiatrist. She was warm and friendly. She didn't just see Demisha as she rested on a cold couch in her office. In fact, Demisha only spent the first two visits in her office. And after those visits, they met at different locations as if they were friends having lunch or something. They met at the coffee shop, the park, and walking trails when it was not cold. Donna believed that different surroundings changed how Demisha felt about things and allowed her to tame her emotions or explode if necessary. Donna was more concerned about Demisha's healing than she was about making money. Sometimes she didn't charge Demisha for the extra time they spent together.

With Donna's help Demisha got through her trauma. Donna was a Christian, and she advised Demisha to attend church to help with her healing process. She knew that only God could help her help Demisha. Donna viewed herself as a vessel that God used to help guide people to God's truth. She often incorporated biblical principles in her counseling, which blew Demisha's mind. Demisha didn't think a psychiatrist would talk about God and the Bible.

After Donna's suggestion, Mel and Demisha vowed to attend church every Wednesday and Sunday. They felt great in church, and the smile that graced Anna's face every time she saw them in church was priceless.

****

They planned for Christmas as usual. Mel's mother was scheduled to come the day after Mike's death, but Mel asked her to postpone her visit because of Mike's death. Since she had taken off for Christmas to come down for Mel and Demisha's wedding, she still came down to meet Demisha and spend Christmas with them.

Mel's mother flew in Christmas day. Everyone was at the house when she came. Mel's mother was 62 years old, but she looked as if she was just turning 50. She wore a chic short haircut that looked very good on her. Her makeup was perfect. Her nails were long, and her hands were full of diamonds. She was just as Demisha had pictured.

Mel took her bags to her room. She spoke to everyone as a whole, and then she excused herself to change into something more comfortable. When she returned she was just as friendly and take charge as she wanted to be. She didn't wait on Mel to introduce her. She introduced herself as she glided across the room.

"Now who is Demisha? I want to meet my new daughter-in-law." She smiled.

Demisha stepped out.

"Mother, this is Demisha, my beautiful wife to be." Mel took her over to Demisha.

"Hi, Mrs. —" Mel's mother interrupted Demisha.

"Beautiful she is! Nice to meet you, Demisha. He did it this time! I can see it in your eyes. Call me Eleanor. You are almost my daughter-in-law

now. Leave all that formalness where it is."
Eleanor darted out. She hugged Demisha tight.

She turned toward Anna. "And who are
you?" Eleanor asked. Her energy burst all over
the place.

"Mother Eleanor, this is Demisha's mother,
Mother Anna." Mel said.

"Well, hi, Mother Anna. It's so nice to meet
you. You give me a hug too because we are days
away from being family. I hope you love my son.
I raised him to be a good man!" Eleanor boasted.

"He is perfect. I couldn't have carved out a
better son-in-law if I tried." Anna attested. "Ya
did a great job."

"Thank you. Thank you." Eleanor said. She
hugged Anna again. "I know you did a great job
too. This is my first time meeting Demisha, but we
have had lovely conversations over the phone.
Haven't we, Demisha?"

"Yes, ma'am." Demisha smiled.

"She is just as beautiful as she sounded over
the phone. They make a beautiful couple."
Mother Eleanor added. She turned toward
Demisha's grandmother. "Okay, who is this?"

"This is Demisha's grandmother,
Grandmother Lenna May." Mel said.

"Hey, darling. You give me a hug, honey.

Bless your heart. You have on more rings than me." Eleanor giggled. Lenna May gave her a hug.

"I like my rings. Some of 'em my children bought me. Some of 'em my husband bought me. He dead nigh. Yeah, he gon to be with the Lawd. He was a good man. A good man they daddy was. Father of all my babies. Mmm ummm. We married young. That's how we di' back in my days. Umm huh, di'nt take me forever." Lenna May said.

"We will all be with God someday. I am happy about that." Eleanor said as she rubbed Lenna May's back. She moved over to the next person.

"This is Donna, a good friend." Mel said.

"Hello, Donna. It is nice to meet you." Eleanor hugged Donna too.

"Thank you. You are beautiful. Just stunning! Mel has talked so much about you that I feel it a pleasure to finally meet you." Donna said.

"Aren't you sweet? I try. I try. He said he talks about me. I didn't believe him." Eleanor teased.

"And last but not least this is Mother Anna's sister, Demisha's aunt, Aunt Kissy May." Mel said.

"I know the routine! Now you give me a hug." Kissy May hugged Eleanor.

"Well, okay then! You catch on fast." Eleanor said humorously. The room filled with laughter.

"My husband couldn't make it y'all. But he will be here for the wedding. I just got married myself six years ago. Did Mel tell you?" Eleanor asked.

"No, ma'am." Demisha answered.

"Mel doesn't tell anyone much. He can't keep up with his mother. I take trips. I do things, baby! I stay young. Mel thinks I stay too young. Don't you, Mel?" She looked at Mel, grabbed his hand, and smiled. Then she continued, "Tell the truth son."

"No, mother, I just like you to take care of yourself." He said.

"I do! By getting up and going! What do you do, Anna? Do you sit and wait in a rocking chair, honey?" Eleanor asked.

"No, I do not! I agree with you." Anna answered.

"That's what I tried to tell Mel. Sitting home makes you old. If I would have been home in my rocking chair like Mel wants me to be, I would have never found that husband I have!" Eleanor said. Everyone laughed.

The time passed so quickly. They didn't have dinner until about ten o'clock that night, and Demisha's family and Donna didn't leave until about one the next morning. Eleanor turned in as soon as everyone left.

Mel and Demisha stayed behind and cleared the table and talked. "Today made me think about Mike. It was just Thanksgiving that he was here with us." Demisha said.

"Yeah, I know." Mel somberly said.

"So, Mel, when are you going to tell her?"

"I don't know. I don't even know how to tell her."

"You know we must tell her. I'm okay with it because irrespective of how she deals with it, I know I have you." Demisha walked over to Mel and put her arms around him.

"Baby, no one could ever turn me against or away from you, not even my mother. I really don't think she will try to turn me against you. She will understand. She's a good person. I know she'll be concerned for me and for you. That's how she is."

"Yeah, but she may not agree with you marrying me. Everyone doesn't know about HIV."

"I think she would totally understand why I love and still choose to marry you."

"Baby, I don't understand. This is not something so simple and easy. I am filled with trepidation. How can you not be?" Demisha paused. "Mel, I don't understand! Why you're still here?" Demisha flopped down in one of the chairs.

Mel bent down in front of the chair that she sat in. He positioned her head up with his hand on her chin, so he could look into her eyes. "Baby, look at me. Just look at me! I am not perfect, and I am still here because of you! I have never found a woman like you! No spirit like yours and never a soul so deep! I have never felt this way about anyone in my life! I wipe your tears away because I know they don't belong there. I kiss where they were because I want to bring happiness to your space. I love you, and I don't want to see your beautiful brown eyes blue. Don't ever wonder why I'm still here. I'm here because I would be lost without you."

Demisha sniffed. "If it was you, I don't know if I would have done the same. I guess I feel guilty because I ask myself that question every day. If your test was the one positive, would I have stayed with you?"

"Okay, listen. It's not me. It's you. Your mother always says that God doesn't put more on you than you can handle. Maybe God didn't allow it to be me because he knew you wouldn't be able to handle it. But I can handle it."

"It doesn't hurt you to know that I am not sure what I would have done if you had been positive?"

"No!" He smirked. "Women always ponder what if. Men deal with what it is. You are HIV positive. I am going to marry you and take you as my wife! That's it! Plain and simple! There is nothing to cry about. Nothing to deliberate over!"

Eleanor entered the kitchen in her robe. "Oh, I'm sorry. Is everything okay?"

"Yes, mother. It's good you're here. I need to talk to you. Demisha, why don't you go upstairs and get yourself ready for bed. Mother can help me down here." Mel said.

"Okay. Goodnight, Mother Eleanor." Demisha kissed her on her cheek.

"Goodnight, Demisha." Eleanor said.

"Do you remember we used to do this together when I was younger?" Mel asked Eleanor.

"Of course I do. This was how we talked about everything that happened in your day. You loved being in the kitchen, so it was never a shock to me when you became a great cook." Eleanor said.

"I do love to cook."

"Demisha is not going to have to worry about anything because I raised a great man."

"Maybe she will have to worry about some things, mother. But I am here to try to make it better."

"What is it, son?"

"Mother, Demisha is sick."

"What's wrong with her?"

"She tested positive for HIV."

"What!"

"Yes."

"Do you have it?"

"No. My test was clean."

"Son, what are you going to do?"

"Well, mother, I'm going to stay with her. I am going to marry Demisha."

"What?"

"Why shouldn't I? My love didn't change. Her HIV status did."

"But, son, you will put yourself at risk. Aren't you afraid?"

"No. There are ways to protect myself, and Demisha and I are going to take all of those precautions."

"Son, this is serious. I don't know much about it. But Cathy, you remember Cathy? Her son died with AIDS. And, son, she said his skin was about to fall off his bones. He dried up like a raisin. She said he wasn't even the same height. I went to the funeral, and he looked like a child. A six-foot man—looked like a child, son! I am not ready to bury you."

"Mother, you won't have to bury me. I will not get it. We are going to be cautious. I can't leave her. She needs me."

"Son, this is not cancer we are talking about here. This is HIV, and it is catchy."

"Mother."

"Have you really thought about this?"

"Yessss, mother! Like you said this is serious. Yes, I have thought about it. I also thought about being without her, and it wasn't pretty. I don't want to be without her."

"You really love her, don't you?" She asked amazed.

"Yes. I have never met a woman that makes me better like Demisha does. Demisha makes me a better man in so many ways. She makes me smile when I don't want to smile. When we first found out about it, I thought about it. I thought about leaving, but Demisha was made for me."

"Well, I don't want to try to tell you what to do but be careful. This is nothing to play with. Wow, I really did raise you to be a great man. I love Demisha. I think you really did well. I just want you to be okay, son. That's all I want!"

"I'm okay with Demisha."

"Well, I'm okay with Demisha too. I remember you didn't like me dating younger men. But did I listen? No, I didn't. You always thought one of them would kill me." She laughed. "I married one, and I am as happy as I can be. So I bless you both. And if you have faith that it is going to be okay, it is going to be okay. You always make great decisions. You have always been a great man."

"Thank you, mother. I needed to hear you say that."

"Well, I am going upstairs back to bed."

"You're not going to help me with the kitchen?"

"Nooo! We used to do this together. Mama done with those days, and I have to get my beauty rest. I just wanted some tea. That's why I got a young husband and a maid. You can handle it. I raised you that way." Eleanor laughed and walked out of the kitchen.

"Demmmisha!" He yelled humorously.

CHAPTER SIX

THE WOMAN WHO GOT BIT BY A SNAKE

My mother had done all the hard work for the wedding, so I really didn't have anything to do. My mother looked forward to me getting married, and she didn't need any help with the planning. She worked even harder after my diagnoses and Mike's death.

I concentrated on getting mentally and physically ready for the wedding, which gave me time to spend with Mel's mother. After hearing the news about my HIV status, Mel's mother decided to stay with us until the wedding. Originally she had planned to leave after Christmas and return in February.

Eleanor and I really had a very good time getting to know each other. She was loving and down-to-earth. For the rest of her visit she and I did so much together. We went to lunch, shopping, a comedy show, and dinner. The only time Mel's mother and I were not together was during my appointments with my psychiatrist. I think Mel got a little jealous.

Mel's mother and I got a chance to talk about my HIV status. I knew the conversation would come up because we were spending so much time together. She and I sat at the coffee shop. Mother Eleanor loved coffee.

"So my son really loves you. You make him happy, and I know why. You are a great girl. You're beautiful too."

"Thank you, Mother Eleanor. Beauty isn't everything though. It fades, and in my condition it may fade faster."

"Don't say that. Mel told me what you are dealing with. How do you feel?"

"Well, I feel blessed to have Mel."

"I mean you. How do you feel?"

"I am okay. I met my Mr. Right and everything was perfect. Then the end of last year a hurricane appeared. My happiness was snatched away. I lost my best friend, and I found out I had a deadly infection. I thought I wasn't going to make it."

"But you made it. God kept you. How long have you been seeing that psychiatrist?"

"Not long—a little over a month. Since I am back at school, I can't see her as much."

"Is she helping?"

"Yes, ma'am, she has helped. She really has. I was skeptical about seeing a psychiatrist, but she is great."

"Nothing wrong with seeing a psychiatrist. God gifted her to do what she does. I got a friend name Shirley who stays in the church, and she will not go to a doctor. Said she has faith that God will heal her."

"What!"

"Ain't nothin' wrong with having faith. I told her God gifted them doctors too. None of us know all things, but God gave us gifts to make his job a little easier. She still sick today. Goin' round to herb shops. I told her don't come over my house with all that coughing. If she gonna be stupid, be stupid at her own house. We too old for her to be so dumb—you know what I am saying. She waited 'til she got up in age to get stupid. Nah, you keep that to yourself. How you gon wait 'til you get 60 to get dumb? I told her somethin' has eaten up her brain cells. 'Cause she get dumber by the minute. It's against the law to be so old and so stupid. I aint makin' the same mistakes at 60 years old that I made when I was 20 years old."

I laughed so hard my eyes started watering.

"I'm serious. She's one of my best friends too. But if she wants to be so holy that she doesn't ever go to the doctor, stay at home. I go to the doctor. It's just like the story I heard one day at church. The pastor said there was this woman that got bit by a poisonous snake. A man came by and told her he needed to suck the poison out so that she wouldn't die. She told the man no because she had faith that God would save her. Another man came by and he told her he needed to suck the poison out before the poison traveled to her heart. She told him no because God would save her. The lady got sicker and sicker. A third man came by and told her he needed to suck the poison out of her leg. She told the third man no. A man that wasn't her husband wasn't going to suck on her leg. God would save her. The poison traveled to the lady's heart, and she died. When she got to heaven she asked God why he didn't save her. God told her he sent three men by to help her, and she turned all three of them down. The moral of the story is, use what you have first."

This old lady was funny. I laughed and laughed. But I never missed the wisdom that was entangled in her humor. "Wow! That is so true."

"Yes, it is. God made us where we all need each other. No doctor is perfect. No pastor is perfect, but God created us all where we need each other. It is a gift to be a doctor. I wasn't created to study as hard as they have to study. Those books they study would drive me nuts. I get to looking at all those words."

"Me too."

"So there is nothing wrong with seeing a psychiatrist. Doctors give you some medicine to take for your sickness, take it. It all works together. Some people God will heal according to their faith. And some people have to utilize the gifts of other people. Nothing wrong with that."

"Donna is Christian too, and she leads her clients to God. She makes it plain and clear that she couldn't do what she does without God."

"See. That is what I am talking about. It all works together. Her and God working together to help you. In my day baby, black people thought it was weak to go see a psychiatrist. Thought only white people did it. That's why a lot of black people messed up today."

"That's true. I never thought about that."

"White people messed us up, baby. We need a psychiatrist. Reparation should be a lifetime of psychiatry treatments for us black folks, umm huh. Counseling! Black people have been through a lot at the hands of white people. We beat our kids because white people used to beat us. Now they lockin' us up for it when they taught us what to do. But I didn't have to beat Mel. White people know they messed us up. There were times we had to do everything on our own. Black people are strong, but now you don't have to do everything by yourself, so don't. It's okay to let someone help you. Ya been through a lot."

"Yes, ma'am. Say that."

"You need to talk everything out sometimes. I know I do."

"Me too. It feels better to get it out. It is such a release."

"At first I didn't know what to say when Mel told me he was still going to marry you. I was scared for him. That's my baby — my only baby!"

"I know. I was scared for him too."

"But Mel always made great decisions. I trust him. He's been precocious all his life. He had so much sense that he scared me sometimes. Boy had more sense than me."

"We are going to take precautions, and we have been counseled about it. So I feel like we are going to be okay."

"That is great. I will be praying for y'all. I have to admit, I wasn't happy at first. But I love you, Demisha. I am glad I stayed on down here and spent this time with y'all. Get to know you."

"I am glad too. I feel like I have a second mother."

"That's good. I'm happy you are comfortable with me. Mel and I just plain ol' people. I didn't have to work hard for what I have." She giggled.

"What?"

"Some people work hard for what they have, and some people marry what they have. I married a rich man, Mel's father. He died, and left me everything. I worked because I wanted too. Now I just travel. My husband now rich too."

"Whaaaaat?"

"Yes, ma'am. I can't have a financially depleted man — broke man. That is why Mel has something going on for himself. I taught him that way."

"Yes, he does. Mel always has something going. He was thinking about opening up a restaurant."

"I know. He has that good touch. He is successful at everything he does. I haven't seen one flop yet. He took after his father."

"He said that."

"He did. I have always been beautiful. I have never been business savvy. I had to learn a little when Mel's father died. People would rip me off. Can't be no dumb woman. But I got smarter and what I didn't know I hired somebody who knew. See, we all work together. God didn't say we had to do it all by ourselves. God created people to help us. You don't have to be ashamed when you need help. But not getting help will make you ashamed. You ready to get up from here?"

"Yes, ma'am, if you are."

"I'm ready. Mel probably wondering about us. His two girls out without him again. I love me some coffee, but I tell you what, it makes me so hot when I drink too much of it."

"Don't worry when we get out in this cold you'll be all right." I giggled.

"I sure will. Atlanta so cold it freezes your nose hairs. Now you know that's cold. Last time I felt cold that froze the hairs in my nose, I was a girl. I thought God didn't make cold like that no mo'. Every time we think we know God he shows us something else, doesn't he?" She chuckled.

I giggled. "You are so funny."

"I'll be funny for sixty-two more years if God allows me to."

CHAPTER SEVEN

HERE COMES THE BRIDE

It was Saturday, February 14, 1998, my wedding day. I anticipated my wedding especially since the only thing I had seen was my wedding dress and my girls' dresses. I also knew the location of the wedding and reception.

Mel's mother and I rode together. I wore jeans and a T-shirt to the church. I would get dressed at the church. When we got to the church, it was breathtaking. My mother had it decorated from top to bottom. It looked like a paradise. Mel's mother and I stood in the entrance of the sanctuary amazed at how beautiful and intricate the decorations were.

"Oh, God! This is magnificent! My mother really did a great job! Wow!" I said with my hands full. The farther we walked into the sanctuary the more ornate it seemed to get.

"Look at the red and white flowers with the silver bows and ribbons. This is beautiful! Big flower arrangements! Love it!" Mother Eleanor said amazed too. "I don't think I have ever seen anything so spectacular!"

"She really did a wonderful job. I never knew my mother did flowers, so the florist probably did this. But my mother did all the planning. I knew she would make sure it was perfect. She added some things to the wedding when we changed the date. Originally, I didn't have any bridesmaids."

"Your mother was waiting on this day, darling! She put her foot in this, as my mother used to say."

The church was large enough to seat 500 hundred people. The ceilings were high and the lights were bright. The flower arrangements were huge and all over the church. She had an arch covered with red and white flowers and silver bows at the top of the altar where Mel and I would stand with the pastor. On the end of every pew, there was a flower arrangement with a black angel inside of the arrangement. It was unbelievable. I couldn't have imagined it if I tried. I had never even seen anything on television like it. My mother exceeded my expectations, especially with the small amount of time she had.

"When will your mother get to the church or is

she already here?" Eleanor asked.

"She should be here in the next ten minutes or so. She's going to help me put on my dress and make sure everyone is okay."

Just after I answered Eleanor, my mother and another lady entered the church. "Speaking of the angel—here she is." Eleanor said.

"Hello, Eleanor. How are you?" My mother hugged Mother Eleanor.

"I am just fine. Looking at this work of art you have done here. Everything is so beautiful. You put your foot in this! I have never seen anything this gorgeous in my life. And I have been to quite a few weddings in my time." Eleanor said.

"Mother, you did such a wonderful job!" I said as she reached over and hugged me.

"I cannot take all the credit. This is the florist right here. This is Helena, and Helena this is my daughter Demisha and her soon to be mother-in-law Eleanor." My mother introduced us.

"Nice to meet you guys, especially the bride. Your mother does not play about what she wants for you. I really enjoyed doing this job. I had to pull out my team, but we are honored that you like it." Helena said smiling.

"We love it! How did you get the angels on the pews to look like they are flying? My God, I have never seen anything like it!" I said.

"I didn't do that part. My assistant Gloria did that, but she used wire to make them sit up and out of the flowers." Helena answered.

"Whose idea was it to put the angels in the flowers? That is different." Eleanor asked.

"That was the bride's mother. She knew what she wanted. She gave me new inspiration." Helena pointed to my mother.

"Wow! I told your daughter you were waiting on this day. Black angels — unbelievable!" Eleanor commented.

"Helena was great! She gave me a great deal on everything. She really is a blessing. I told her the time we were working with, and she got right on it." My mother shared.

"It's beautiful, Ms. Helena. I love it! I knew my mother would have it together! She always does! This is her day just as much as it is mine." I hugged Ms. Helena.

"No problem. I love my job. My clients bring out the best in me as I give them the best." Helena said.

"Mother, you look beautiful too. I love your skirt suit, so you got dressed at home." I said.

"Yes, I have to help you dress. I wouldn't have time for me. This is your day, so I did my little stuff at home." My mother said.

My mother looked stunning. She had on a beautiful red satin skirt suit with some red satin heels. She had a white corsage embellished with red and silver ribbon. She wore her hair in a classic bun and spiraled curls. And she had lost about twenty pounds.

"Here comes Barbara and some of the other girls who are in the wedding. Let me lead y'all to the dressing room. Helena, ya can help me get the girls and Mother Eleanor situated in the dressing room." My mother said jumping in facilitator mode.

"Okay." Helena replied.

Mother led us all to the dressing room. I felt nervous. It was really happening. I was getting married.

"I am feeling nervous." I said aloud but unaware that I had.

"It's okay, child. You're supposed to be nervous about now. You think you are nervous now, wait until those guests start piling in the church." Mother Eleanor said as she rubbed my shoulder.

Once I got into the dressing room I felt better because mother had refreshments there for us. She thought of everything. It took us all about 45 minutes to get dressed. We had no idea what was going on in the church.

The guys got dressed down the hall from us. I had not seen Mel in two days; he stayed with my mother. I really wanted to see him. I tried to imagine him. I had no idea how his tuxedo looked.

****

Finally everything was in place, and the wedding ceremony began. Everything started on time. My mother was the timekeeper, and she was never late. The girls left out first. I waited for my cue as I sat in the dressing room with the assistant director Van, who is one of my mother's closest friends. I looked beautiful just as I had imagined. My dress was a soft ivory. It hugged every curve I had in my body. Rhinestones shined from it; they looked like real diamonds. The train was not very long, but it fanned out at the bottom. Connecting the train to the dress was a beautiful ivory satin bow with rhinestones covering it, and on the outside of the train was a silver line tracing the entire train. The line sparkled.

I wore a tiara headpiece — something a queen would wear. Ivory chiffon cascaded down my back. My face was uncovered, and my makeup was perfect. I had my makeup artist come in to do the entire bridal party. Needless to say, everyone had fabulous makeup.

I sparkled as I sat stiff as a tree — afraid to move. I didn't want to mess up anything. I looked picturesque. "Okay, come on out it is almost time for your entrance." Van said. She stood halfway in and halfway out of the dressing room door in order to get her cue. My uncle Bob walked down to my dressing room door. He took my hand and placed it in the bend of his arm. "Ya look beautiful my little knucklehead." He kissed my cheek.

"Thanks, Uncle Bob. You don't look too shabby yourself. That working out has been doing you good." I facetiously said. But he did look very handsome in his tuxedo, and I loved my uncle Bob. He had been there for me throughout my life. He was the only man worthy of walking me down the aisle.

As we walked down the hall to the entrance of the church sanctuary, I did everything I could to hold back my tears. I didn't want to ruin my makeup. We paused near the sanctuary doors. I couldn't wait to see Mel. I missed him so. He was all that was on my mine until the doors to the entrance of the sanctuary flew open, and I saw all the guests turn toward Uncle Bob and me.

Everyone stood to their feet. Some of their mouths dropped. I was a little nervous. The piano played as Uncle Bob and I walked slowly. I looked straight ahead blocking everyone out. The aisle seemed to get longer and longer until I saw this bright light. The light was almost blinding, and below it stood Mel, my angel. We both smiled at each other as he stood in place watching Uncle Bob and I walk down the aisle. Mel was mesmerized by my beauty. His eyes gleamed. He looked very handsome in his black penguin tail tuxedo.

I remember seeing his groomsmen briefly. The guests in the church reappeared. It was packed. There were people standing against the walls. Although I didn't return on a regular basis until Donna suggested I should, this was my home church. My mother had been a faithful member there for over 49 years. So she knew everyone, and she invited everyone. Mel and his mother invited over 200 hundred people. I never dreamt of having so many people at my wedding. But no matter how many people were there, one very important person wasn't there, Mike.

Finally, Uncle Bob and I made it to the altar. Mel looked very anxious to get next to me. The music on the piano stopped, and everyone faced the pastor. The pastor walked closer and stood in front of Uncle Bob and me.

"Beautiful, beautiful bride you have here." The pastor said as she turned to Mel. Mel smiled.

"We are all gathered here today to witness the union of this man and this woman. Who give this woman to be taken in holy matrimony by this man?" The pastor asked.

"I do." Uncle Bob answered boldly and then handed my hand to Mel. Uncle Bob kissed my cheek and took his seat. I turned just a little to see

Uncle Bob sit down. When I looked I saw my mother, and I smiled at her. Next to her was an empty chair with a beautiful flowered sign with Mike's name on it in silver sparkling ribbon. My eyes watered up. Mike was there with me. What my mother did was so special and innovative. I never saw anyone save an empty chair for someone deceased at a wedding. My mother thought of everything. My nerves immediately dissipated when I saw Mike's chair.

"Let us say a prayer for this beautiful couple. Place your hands in this Bible Demisha and Mel. Please get your rings too." I reached over to Stacy for Mel's ring, and Mel reached over to his best man Claude for my ring. We placed the rings in the Bible along with our hands. We bowed our heads and the pastor prayed.

"God, we thank you for blessing us all to get here safely to witness in the uniting of two souls. This man and this woman — in holy matrimony. And we pray that we can have many more great unions to follow this one. God, we ask you to bless this couple to share a beautiful life together. Bless one to be strong where the other is weak. Bless their union to be holy and unique. And just as the decorations are filled with angels, let them walk out of here with angels guarding them wherever they go. Let your will be done for their lives. In Jesus mighty-mighty name we pray. Let the church say Amen."

"Amen." The church said almost in unison.

"Do you Melvin Underwood take Ms. Demisha Coleman to be your lawfully wedded wife in sickness and in health, through sunshine and rain, and aging and change?"

"I do." Mel answered looking into my eyes. His eyes were so glossy. He worked hard to restrain his tears.

"Ms. Demisha Coleman, do you take Mr. Melvin Underwood to be your lawfully wedded husband in sickness and in health, through sunshine and rain, and aging and change?"

"I sure do. I do!" I said energetically. Laughter sprouted throughout the church.

"Then by the power bestowed upon me I now pronounce you husband and wife. You may kiss your bride." The pastor said.

Mel grabbed me and kissed my lips. It was a long kiss too. I heard people laughing and cheering.

After our kiss the pastor presented us to the congregation. "What God has brought together no man shall put asunder. I now introduce to you Mr. and Mrs. Melvin and Demisha Underwood."

The church stood up and clapped, and the piano played. It was one of the happiest days of my life. I was finally a wife. I was a wife and not someone's bridesmaid or guest.

The wedding reception was immediately following the wedding at the Sumerou Hotel. We had such a wonderful time. My mother had everything stunning. My wedding cake had seven tiers. They were white with red roses on them and underneath the cake was a sparkling fountain. And to the left of my cake was Mel's cake, a square two-layered chocolate cake with fresh fruit on top. I don't know who catered, but the food was delicious. I wouldn't have changed anything.

Everyone danced and celebrated all night long. Mel and I partied about three hours, and then we left everyone else behind. We had to get ready to leave that next morning for our honeymoon. We honeymooned in Miami, Florida for three days and two nights. We decided against honeymooning in the Islands because I had to return to school.

CHAPTER EIGHT

MRS. UNDERWOOD

I returned to school after our honeymoon. I missed my students, and they seemed to have missed me too. They asked me so many questions when I returned. They were aware that I had gotten married. Some of their parents made the wedding.

"Ms. Coleman, what is your new name since you married?" Jose asked.

"Now I am Mrs. Underwood." I said as I wrote on the board.

"Mrs. Underwood, right?" David asked.

"Yes, that's right." I responded.

David continued. "Why ya been gone so long? We missed ya and thought ya were not coming back."

"Well, I got married and had to take a honeymoon. But it was only a few days, David. I missed you guys too. My husband wanted to have a longer honeymoon, but I wanted to get back to you."

"We sure missed ya, Ms. Coleman." Tonia added.

"It's Mrs. Underwood now, stupid. Don't you see it on the board?" Jacob corrected her.

"Okay, that is enough. No one is stupid in here. It may take some time getting used to my new name, and that is all right."

"Mrs. Underwood, what is a honeymoon?" Saedie asked.

"It's like a vacation that husbands and wives take." I answered.

"Oh! My mother and father take those every year." Saedie said. "Sometimes I go too."

"The other teacher couldn't play the noun game like ya did. And she said we had to wait 'til ya come back because she didn't know what we were talking 'bout." Tonia informed me.

"She didn't know the game because I created it. I'm back now, and I won't be going anywhere else until school is out for spring and summer. When I break so will you guys, and we will all come back together."

"Mrs. Underwood, when is school out? I said her name right." Betty said.

"For spring—in April and for summer June 6th. I think. I will check to make sure. Why? Are you ready to get out of school already, Betty?"

"I just asked because my birthday is when school is out." Betty answered.

"Oh, please not your birthday again, Betty. You love birthdays, huh?" I asked.

"Yes, ma'am. I love parties too. My mama always gives good parties." Betty smiled.

"I love parties too." I smiled.

I had twenty kids in my first grade class this year, and they all gathered around me at this long table we had in the classroom. My students were like my very own children. I loved them, and they loved me. I didn't have a problem child in the bunch, but I knew how to love and teach the problem children too. It was all a part of being a teacher.

At the end of the day I felt extremely exhausted. I forgot to take my vitamins that the doctor prescribed for me since my diagnoses. I took one as soon as I thought about it, but it was too late. I felt okay once I got into the truck. But after about five minutes of driving I didn't feel so well. I felt dizzy. I went to my mother's house to lie down for a moment because her house was closer to the school.

My mother wasn't home, so I used my key to

get in. I stretched out across her sofa because I was too lightheaded to go upstairs. I never felt weak before, and I knew it was because of the virus that I did then. It seemed that getting tested and finding out I had the virus made me develop symptoms. I seemed fine before I was tested and never once had any symptoms of sickness. I got tired sometimes, but I blamed it on age before I knew I had the virus.

"Demisha! Demisha." Mel shook my arm.

"Huh." I said not quite awake.

"Come on, baby, wake up. Let's go home." Mel said. I opened my eyes and sat up. My mother stood on the other side of Mel.

"I came home about four o'clock and found ya on the sofa asleep. I left ya sleeping. I put a spread over ya, and I called Mel at the store. Didn't want him worryin' about ya." My mother said.

"Why you didn't go home, baby? Anything wrong?" Mel asked.

"I was a little tired. I couldn't make it that far, baby."

"Did you take your vitamins the doctor gave you?" Mel asked looking as if he already knew the answer.

"I forgot, but I took them when I started feeling tired?"

"Baby, you can't forget to take your vitamins! You must take your vitamins. Even if you have to set your watch to remind you, then that's what you do." He lifted me up from the sofa.

"Okay, I will. I will." I said.

"I was worried about you because before mother called me I called home, and you were not there." Mel said.

"What time is it?" I asked.

"It's a little after seven. I let you get ya rest because I knew for ya to come here ya had to be tired." My mother said.

"Well, we have two cars now. And I still don't feel like driving." I said.

"You don't have to. I got our neighbor to drop me off because I knew if you had come here and fell asleep you would not be prepared to drive. So I don't have the car. I will drive the truck." Mel said.

"Mel, you think of everything. God put you in her life for a reason greater than we knew." Mother rubbed Mel's back.

"Thank you, mother. But Demisha is the prize, my prize. And that's why she better do everything she can to remember to take her meds."

"I will, I will. Okay, mother, we will see you later." I said.

She walked us to the door. She kissed Mel and me. "I love you two. Demisha, make sure you take your vitamins. Make sure you take anything the doctor gives you! Anything!" She said.

"I will, mother. I will."

When Mel and I got home we ate dinner. "You must have cooked dinner before you came to get me?" I asked.

"Yes. I figured you would be hungry, so I made something quick before I got the neighbor to drop me off. How was your day?"

"It was good. The kids asked me so many questions. What was my new name? What was a honeymoon? I gave them their little goodie-bags after lunch. I told them you helped make them. They cannot wait to meet you."

"The kids want to meet me? Kids are grown nowadays. When I was a kid we didn't care anything about our teacher's husband. We didn't even see our teacher as a regular person."

"How was your day at the store?"

"It was okay. I didn't stay all day at the store. I transferred my calls to my cell phone. That is how mother got in touch with me. I went to look at some property this man wants to sell."

"Where?"

"Near the West End Mall. It's an old house that I could probably work on and make it out of a rooming house. What do you think?"

"I don't know. You know I am not too much on business. If it's a good investment you should go for it and make it work. How much is he selling it for?"

"$60,000. He wants $8,000 down and $350 a month."

"Is that good? I know it sounds good."

"It's very good. After I fix the house it will be worth so much more than $60,000. I will do the work myself, so I will only spend about $15,000 to bring it up to standard. The house has five rooms and a basement. I can rent the basement out for $1000 a month if I fix it up right. Then each room for $500 a month furnished. So basically it pays for itself and puts money in our pockets. With paying the mortgage and the utilities every month, I will recover the $15,000 in less than two years. Not to change the subject but I want you to seriously set your watch for your meds. I don't want anything to happen to you while you're driving home."

"I know, I know. But I forgot, and you and Mother are acting as if I committed a crime!"

"I don't mean to sound that way. But this is about your health, and I am very concerned. I don't want to have to wonder whether you made it home or not. Now enough of that because I don't want to make you upset. Tomorrow I am taking us out. I want to see that new movie that's out."

"What movie? Love story?"

"I don't remember the name, but Denzel is starring in it."

"Okay. We both know I love some Denzel. Going to a movie on a weeknight always gives me energy."

"Oh, Donna called you earlier when I was home cooking dinner. She wants to know when you're going to start back seeing her. I told her that you would call her once you got in."

"Yes, I will call her. I think I will start back seeing her next week. I haven't talked to Donna since the wedding reception."

"Well, don't take up any of my time seeing her."

"I won't." I smiled. "I actually want us to start seeing her friend who is a marriage counselor."

"Us! Why? We don't have any problems."

"Yeah, I know. But Donna said that all married couples should see a counselor their entire marriage at least once or twice a month when there are no problems and more when there are problems. She said it keeps a healthy marriage healthy. I think she is right. Seeing a counselor will give us a way to talk about things that may be hard for us to discuss one on one. Relationships incur changes, so I think we should do whatever we can to make sure ours continue to thrive."

"I am down for whatever. Anything if they can get you to take your meds. I think the honeymoon really did us both some good. That made me ready for the next vacation."

"The wedding too. I felt like I was in heaven. Anything that was bothering me was released as soon as I walked in those sanctuary doors."

"I know. I felt the same way. Your mother did a great job. Whenever I want to do something else, I am going to give her the money and tell her to go to work. She was amazing. She will earn my money from now on for any event I am planning. If I buy that house, I will pay her to pick out the furniture and decorate it."

"I didn't know my mother was capable of all of that. Really — I had no idea. I am still shocked. Our wedding looked as if it took years to plan."

CHAPTER NINE

THE BIG 40

Two years later

Mel and I were doing great together. I couldn't have asked for a better husband. My health began to deteriorate a little. The doctor put me on more medication. I didn't know why because I really didn't take the first set of pills he gave me. That's probably why my health started to deteriorate. I wasn't trying to be defiant by not taking the medicine. The medicine made me sick. I hated swallowing so many pills, and once I swallowed them they made me feel worse. So just like the first set of pills the doctors gave me, I occasionally took the second set of medicine. It was no fun being sick all the time from medicine that was supposed to make you better. It didn't make any sense to me. I had enough pills to start a pharmacy. It was ridiculous.

I stopped seeing Donna about a few months after Mel and I were married. She and I continued being friends. We often met for lunch and sometimes did a movie. She recommended Mel and me to her friend for marriage counseling. Mel and I saw him once a month for two hours just to maintain a healthy marriage.

Mel worries about me a lot. A patch of his black hair in the front turned snow white. It only makes him look more distinguished, but I don't like him worrying about me. He claims that his hair turning white in the front has nothing to do with worrying.

I tried so hard to cover up my health as it began to deteriorate, but Mel watched me like a hawk whenever I was home. I lost twenty pounds, and my appetite was not good at all. I ate a lot of fruit and raw vegetables to sustain me. I didn't look unhealthy. For someone just meeting me, I looked extremely fit.

My mother was very strong or at least that was all she showed me. I knew that the changes she saw me experiencing made her scared. I think she tried hard to accept that maybe I was going to die before her. She stayed full of joy whenever she was around me. Never did I see her cry or mourn as if I was already dead.

I turned 40 years old, and I felt great about myself. Mel and I couldn't do anything on my birthday because I had to work. But he promised to take me somewhere that Saturday.

When Saturday came, Mel awoke early. When I turned over and reached for him he was gone. It startled me because when I looked at the clock it was only seven o'clock in the morning.

"Mel!" I sprouted out of bed. I grabbed my

robe that was in the chair next to the bed. I walked downstairs. "Mel!"

"What, baby? I'm here. What's wrong?" He answered. He met me at the stairs.

"Nothing, I just missed you. Why are you up so early?"

"I had a few things to do. I ran mother a couple of places too."

"This early! Where did she need to go this early? That means you have been gone at least two hours, and I didn't know it."

"Baby, she's got something she's going to do later. She has a new boyfriend who she wants to cook dinner for, and she wants us to meet him later."

"My mother has a new boyfriend, and she didn't tell me! I don't believe it!"

"Well, believe it because I think she really likes him. She wanted to keep it as a surprise for you, but since you awoke and I wasn't in bed I had to tell you the truth."

"No, I can't believe my mother. I'm not some little kid that she has to hide things from me. I noticed that lately she has been whispering a lot!"

"Come on, let's eat. Breakfast is ready. We can talk about that later."

I took a seat at the table. "I don't know if I feel

like eating so early. I am sorry for raising my voice, but my mother and I have always been close. I can't believe she has a new boyfriend and didn't tell me."

"Baby, maybe she thinks it will be better if she surprises you. Don't take it so personal because now you are acting like the little kid that you said you were not."

"No, you —" Mel stuck a biscuit into my mouth. Mel started laughing. I removed the biscuit. "You are not funny, Mel! And you know I can't eat this."

"Try, baby. You ate some bread the other day. Look, I just don't want you to make a big deal out of mother and her new boyfriend. You don't need any stress. I got a surprise for you."

"What kind of surprise? Between you and my mother I don't know if I like your surprises. I think I need to know upfront what's going on. Y'all have too many secrets for me." I rolled my eyes and nibbled on my biscuit.

"I just want to take you somewhere special. Since your birthday fell on a weekday, today I want to do a little som' somthin for you. So I have a little something up my sleeves."

"Oh, how sweet. Let me eat my breakfast and be good then. My baby wants to do something special for me." I put more food in my mouth. "I don't think my mother supposed to have a boyfriend anyway. She is a minister now. When did ministers start having boyfriends?"

"Ministers have boyfriends. They just don't have sex with them, but how are they going to get married if they don't have a boyfriend first? You are just spoil and don't want to admit it. When it comes to your mother you think you are supposed to know everything."

"That is not true. Ministers don't have boyfriends."

"What if she would have told you that when you told her about me?"

"I wasn't in church like she is. When I met you I never portrayed myself as a saint, and you know it. My mother knew I was no saint. Every time I went to the club she knew about it. She didn't know about my escapades and rendezvous but no mother should. I thank God for where I am today. I am not what I want to be, but I am sure not what I used to be. I have come a long way. I never thought I would be here."

"You are too funny. Eat your breakfast so we can get our day started. You-ah big baby." Mel giggled.

Mel and I left the house about one o'clock that afternoon. We dressed casual. Mel didn't want us to dress up. It was a nice and hot day out. Spring was officially two days away. We took the truck. He was supposed to be driving to an undisclosed location. However, after we exited the highway, I noticed that we were headed toward my mother's house.

"Why are we going to mother's house?"

"I left something over there when I dropped her off. Something I need to make sure our day goes well." He explained.

"You left your wallet?"

"Yeah. How did you know?" He giggled.

"Because you said we couldn't get our day started without it. I told you about that wallet. You need to put it on a string around your neck. I hope the cops don't stop us. Driving without a license."

We pulled up into my mother's driveway and got out of the truck.

"We are not staying because I have plans for us. We will come back and meet mother's boyfriend."

"Yeah and I am going to tell my mother about herself too. How could she not tell me about her little boyfriend and tell you! I smell barbecue. Mel, don't you smell barbecue? I know she is not barbecuing and didn't invite me because of her little boyfriend. She's probably barbecuing for her little boyfriend." I ranted as I walked up the driveway to her door.

I stuck my key into her door and stepped into the house. I was startled by a crowd of people. "Surprise!" They yelled.

Mel stood behind me. So when I leaned back he caught me.

"Oh, my God! I can't believe this!" I turned around and looked at Mel. "Mel, you knew all the time!" I smiled.

He kissed my cheek and removed the key out of the door. My mother walked out to the front of the crowd. She wrapped her arms around me and gave me a big hug.

"I can't believe you hid this from me. You did a good job! So you don't have a new boyfriend?" I asked my mother.

"Child, who told ya that?" She rose up from our hug.

"I guess it was just Mel's little plan." I said.

"Okay everyone to the back again!" My mother yelled. There were a few of my co-workers there, Donna, all of my family in Atlanta, Stacy and Cameron, my new neighbors, and Mel's mother and stepfather. I was really shocked when I saw Mel's mother and stepfather because I knew they had to fly in town to be there.

When I got to the backyard, Uncle Bob was manning the grill. There were balloons everywhere, and it was decorated nicely. My mother had found another calling, event planning and decorating. There was a DJ, and he played upbeat gospel music and gospel rap. Everyone danced all over the place. There were plenty of food, non-alcoholic drinks, and fun.

After a while my mother brought out this huge chocolate cake with one candle lit — the number 40.

"Okay, okay, now it is time for the birthday girl to blow out the candle and make a wish! Come on everyone, gather around the birthday girl!" Mother yelled.

I sat down in a chair at the table. I glowed from ear to ear like a little kid. Everyone gathered around and sung happy birthday in unison like they had been practicing it. My mother's doing — I was sure of it.

Mother leaned down near me. "Blow out the candle, baby, and make a wish. Wish for anything ya want."

For a second I blocked out everyone and thought about something I really wished for at that point, life. I stared at the lit candle, and then I made my wish and blew out the candle. Everyone clapped and cheered. If no one else knew what I had wished for, I was sure my mother knew. The DJ turned the music back up, and everyone began to dance and party again.

I stood up and grabbed hold of Mel. "You having a good time?" Mel asked.

"Of course I am. I am just glad my mother doesn't have a new boyfriend." I giggled.

Mother was near us.

"She was hot when I told her you had a new boyfriend and that you wanted to surprise her with him. My mother wouldn't hide anything from me. I am not some kid. We never hide anything from each other." Mel said mocking me to my mother. We all laughed.

"Ya know I would tell my baby if I had a boyfriend. Preachers don't have boyfriends anyway. We have husbands." Mother said.

"That is what I told Mel." I said.

"How will you ever get married if you don't have a boyfriend first? Preachers have to have someone too." Mel said.

"Well, you can date. If ya are dating someone ya like, ya keep dating them until they propose I guess. But I don't like the term boyfriend for me. I don't think I would ever take a man to church and introduce him to my pastor as my boyfriend." Mother said.

"If you date him over and over again that's a boyfriend to me." Mel giggled.

"I don't know. Boyfriend sounds like some benefits are going on." Mother replied.

"Exactly. I told Mel. I knew you hadn't

changed overnight." I said.

"She didn't know anything. I got her good. She was livid." Mel giggled.

"Okay. I am going in to get some more drinks. Get ya guys some cake. Sister Marciela is cutting it for ya." Mother said.

We didn't leave the party until about ten o'clock that night, almost nine hours! Mel and I vowed that after church on Sunday we would stay home and rest.

****

Monday when I went to work I was in a very good mood that resulted from my birthday celebration. When I walked into the front office to sign in, there were several teachers in the office. One particular teacher who was a good friend of mine and had attended my party was in the crowd. Everyone stared at me and stopped talking. I thought it was sort of weird, but I just proceeded to sign in. When I looked up they turned away. I walked to the other side of the office to check my mailbox and all the teachers scattered about except my friend.

"Angela, what is with them?" I asked.

"Well everyone is scared, Demisha."

"Scared of what, girl?"

"Scared of you?"

"Who am I? Last time I checked I wasn't Mike Tyson. Why are they scared of me?" I asked clueless.

"Demisha, everyone knows."

"Everyone knows what, Angela?"

"Everyone knows what is going on. They know that you have AIDS."

I stood totally still for a brief minute. I couldn't believe she said those words. I really didn't know what to say.

"Demisha, I heard someone at your party talking about it. Demisha, you're sick, and you have been walking around here like everything is okay. Everyone had a right to know, and they have a right to be afraid. You may infect one of us or perhaps the children. I knew something was wrong with you when you lost all of that weight. You need to quit, go home, and stay around the people who are not afraid of you." Like a sword, Angela cut me to pieces.

She left me speechless. I thought she was a friend, and in minutes she gutted me like a fish. I was so hurt that I walked swiftly out of the front door toward my car. And the closer I got to the car, I started to run. It seemed the more I ran the farther the car was. I cried, and then I just fell to my knees. I screamed uncontrollably. I literally crawled to my car and unlocked the door.

Once in my car, I tried to stick the key into the

ignition, and it took me two minutes to get the key into the ignition. I was frazzled. I got the car started, gathered my composure, and drove away. All I could envision was Angela telling those teachers I had AIDS without asking me was it true. She looked at me as if I was a child molester. I thought I would die if I stood there any longer.

When I got home Mel wasn't home. He had left for work. It was good he had. At that moment I didn't feel like being cheered up. I felt like crying, and Mel didn't let me do that much. He didn't like to see me sad. I cried myself to sleep. I slept so long that when Mel arrived home later that evening I was still asleep.

"Baby, is everything okay?" He shook me awake.

"Oh, you're home. Baby, I'm so glad you're home." I reached up and grabbed hold of him.

"Why are your stockings torn at the knee? And your skin is broken! What happened?"

I started crying. "Baby, today Angela and the other teachers were all in a huddle when I walked in the office this morning to sign in. Baby, she told all the teachers I have AIDS!"

"What! You don't have AIDS, so she doesn't know anything! There is a difference. How did she find out something was wrong with your health anyway?"

"She said she overheard someone talking

about it at the party. Baby, she cut me down as if I was a child molester or something! She told me I should quit and stay home around people who are not afraid of me! That's what she said! She was really cold, and she didn't show any concern for my feelings."

Mel pressed my head against his chest. "Baby, it's going to be okay. It's going to be okay. What happened to your stockings and your knees? Let me get some peroxide and bandages."

"I ran out the building, and I fell down. I didn't even try to get up, I crawled to my car."

"You did what? Are you okay? I know you're not okay, but you're safe now. You're home. Don't worry about that damn woman! She was probably jealous of you anyway. She laughed in your face, but she was waiting on something to tear you down with! I'll be back." Mel went to get some things to clean my knees.

Mel walked back into the room. "You didn't feel your knees bleeding? I won't bandage it now because I am going to run you a bath."

"She talked about the weight I lost and everything. She said she knew something was wrong. She may have come to the party to snoop. Why did she have to hurt me? I treated her good, baby!"

"I know, Demisha. I know. Everything is going to be okay. Hold your knees up. You don't have to go back there if you don't want to."

"It's my job! I have to go back. I called the principal. I told her I got ill, and I had to leave."

"Well, you just ignore the teacher."

"I can't ignore her. She has told all the other teachers about my illness."

"Well, you fight! Don't let someone make you give up something you love. It doesn't matter with me because we don't need your income, but you love your students because they bring you joy."

"Everyone thinks I will cause them harm or put them at risk of getting the disease. That's what she said."

"Look, I am going to run you a nice bath, bring you dinner, and then I want you to rest. We will not let these people hinder us. There is no way! We have come too far. She is a teacher, and she is still ignorant about HIV? We are in the 21st century. She has the illness if you ask me! She has not educated herself. That's her fault."

"She was so bold to talk to me like she did. Normally, I would have stood up for myself. Baby, I didn't want to fight because I knew she was right."

"She wasn't right! Don't say that! Have you taken your medicine?"

"No. Baby, may I skip it tonight? Sometimes that medicine upsets my stomach so bad that I cannot sleep."

"Okay, just this one time because I really want you to get some rest tonight. But you need your medicine. That medicine will allow you to live a long time. If you love me you will take your medicine."

The next morning as I got dressed I was very nervous. I looked in the mirror wondering how would I return to school and act as if nothing had happened. But I knew I had to go back because Mel was right. I couldn't let anyone hinder my life. I had come too far to allow one person to stop me. Yet, I knew I had so far to go.

"Baby, I have got to go, and don't you be late. Listen, if you need me call me on my cell phone, and I will be there. It's going to be okay." Mel stood behind me with his arms wrapped around my waist.

"Thank you, Mel."

"Okay, baby. I've got to go." He said as he released me.

I looked out of the bedroom window as he drove away.

When I pulled into the school parking lot I cut the car off and said a brief prayer but a very much-needed one. After my prayer I opened my eyes and got out of the car with my things. The front door of the school was about fifty feet away from the teacher's parking lot. I walked toward the school with my head up high and my back straight. "They are not going to tear me down." I said aloud.

At the door I took a deep breath, and then I pulled the door open. There were a lot of teachers going in and out of the office signing in. I walked by a few of them, and I got some stares. Some of the teachers spoke to me and some didn't. But I walked right into the office to sign in and check my mailbox.

I passed Angela as I walked into the office. She gave me a condescending look. I didn't say a word. I didn't have to because I allowed my eyes to do the talking. She wasn't about to make me lower my head.

After signing in at the office, I went to my class and waited for my students to come in from breakfast. My disease didn't impede my teaching. I was a great teacher, and I loved my students. My students loved me.

CHAPTER TEN

TROUBLE BREWING ON THE SCHOOLYARD

Two weeks later

I stood in class preparing my students for a little quiz that I wanted to give them when one of the teachers' assistants walked into the room.

"This is for you. The principal wants to see you, and she sent me here to watch your class until you return." She handed me a white folded piece of paper.

"Okay. Well, class I have to be excused for one minute. Please go over this material with them until I get back. They have a quiz." I handed the assistant the folder with the review questions for the quiz.

"Okay." She said and took a seat in my chair.

I walked right down to the office. I read the paper as I walked, and all it said was the same thing the assistant said to me. I walked into the office and spoke to the secretary. "Hi, Mrs. Wells."

"How are you doing, Mrs. Underwood?" Mrs. Wells asked. "Enjoying the married life?"

"I am fine, and the married life is a dream." I smiled. "I didn't know it could be so great."

"Well, that is great. Mrs. Bird is expecting you." Mrs. Wells said.

I knocked at Mrs. Bird's door. "Come on in." She said.

"Hi, Mrs. Bird. You wanted to see me?" I closed her door behind me.

"Mrs. Underwood, have a seat. How are you doing today?" Mrs. Bird asked.

"Mrs. Bird, I am doing well. How about you?"

"Great. I wanted to talk to you about something I heard."

"What is it?"

"Mrs. Underwood, you know that you are one of the best teachers that I have. Parents love you. The kids love you. But I was told that you are living with a deadly communicable disease. Is this true?" Mrs. Bird boldly asked me.

"Mrs. Bird, who told you this? I don't think I have to discuss my private life with you." I said.

"I will not divulge my source, but Mrs. Underwood it is important that I know the truth. The person that told me is very concerned for his or her life and the lives of the children you teach."

"Please tell me that you are kidding me? This is the 21st century. You mean to tell me that people are still dumb! I can't give those children anything! Those children are my world! I would do anything for each and every one of them! I would never risk those kids!" I was furious.

"So it's true—you're living with AIDS! Oh my." Mrs. Bird said.

"It's HIV. There's a difference! Mrs. Bird, I do my job. My personal life is none of your business."

"Oh, but it is, Mrs. Underwood. I have a teacher threatening to go to the press and the parents of this school. Now I have to fight a battle that I don't think I'm equipped to fight."

"Are you saying my job is at risk?"

"No, I am not saying that. You know that I respect you. I will protect you the best that I can. You are a wonderful teacher and a wonderful human being. You have been with me longer than any other teacher here."

"Do I need to contact my lawyer?"

"No, this is what I don't want to happen. I don't want to get lawyers, television stations, and parents involved. I want this thing to stay small."

"Well, how are we going to do that when you say that you have a teacher threatening you? I want to make sure I am protected. Somehow my privacy has already been invaded."

"I don't know how the teacher found out, but she did. I will handle this. You can go back to your class. You don't have to worry. You are one of my best teachers. I will protect you." Mrs. Bird assured me.

When I got home that evening I decided to cook dinner for Mel and me. My day at school wasn't the best, and I just wanted to relax. When Mel walked into the house he was surprised by the smell of food in the air.

"Hi, baby." I kissed his cheek.

"Hey, how was your day? It had to be good—

you are cooking." Mel said.

"Not good at all, baby. Someone told the principal that I am HIV positive. It just keeps getting worse and worse. I know it was Angela. The first time the principal said he or she, and then the second time she said she. It was Angela."

"What? This woman again! She is very vindictive!"

"Yes, she is. I was so good to her when she was new to Atlanta."

"Well, it doesn't matter who told what. My concern is you. What is the school's concern about you having HIV?"

"Right now Mrs. Bird doesn't want me to be concerned. She said that she is going to protect me. I believe her. I have been with her from the beginning. I was there when she became principal."

"Do you need to contact your lawyer?"

"Not now, she doesn't want to make it bigger than what it is. Go wash up, dinner is ready."

"Well, baby, sometimes you have to be prepared anyway. I know Mrs. Bird is a nice woman, and you have known her a long time. But whose butt do you think she will protect if it came to yours and hers? Hers! We will hold off for now, but you be prepared to do whatever you have to do. You see how Angela did you, and you thought you knew her." Mel walked away to wash his hands. After washing his hands he walked back into the dining room. "Listen, I just don't want you to get hurt. You have been hurt enough. You have to strike sometimes before they strike. Remember that." Mel sat at the table.

"You're right, but I am so tired of fighting."

"Baby, don't ever get tired of fighting. Life is a fight. That is why I am a successful businessman today. I fight hard."

"Baby, I am not you."

"You have always been tough and spicy. Don't allow this little three letter acronym to take the fight out of you! You are still Demisha!"

CHAPTER ELEVEN

TWO BY TWO THEY WENT

ONE WEEK LATER

I was bombarded by a reporter one morning at school. "Are you Demisha Coleman?" He asked stretching out his microphone to my mouth.

"Yes. I am." I answered as I continued walking.

"Is it true, ma'am, that you are teaching the kids here at Milton Academy putting them at risk of contracting HIV?" He trotted alongside me.

"No, it is not true. I am not putting my kids in risk of anything! I love those kids!"

"So you do have HIV, ma'am?"

"Sir, will you please leave me alone!"

"One of the teachers here told us that you're risking her life and the children's lives that you come in contact with every day. How do you feel about that?" He held the microphone toward my mouth.

"Sir, it is the 21st century, anyone who is still ignorant about HIV is living under a rock." I walked swiftly hoping to lose him.

He stopped following me. "They are not under a rock, ma'am. They are at your school. They are at your school!" The reporter yelled.

I hurried into the building. I stormed into the front office very upset. I raced pass Mrs. Wells.

"Mrs. Bird is in her office with someone!" Mrs. Wells stood up and said.

"I don't care!" I said.

"You can't go in there!" Mrs. Wells shouted.

I barged into Mrs. Bird's office. "What is the press doing outside?"

"Mrs. Underwood, you can't just come into my office!" Mrs. Bird stood up from her desk.

"You told me you were going to handle this!"

"I am trying too!"

"Try harder!"

Angela stood up from her chair and turned around to face me. "Why should she be concerned with you? She has an entire school to be concerned about!" She was the person Mrs. Bird was talking to before I barged into Mrs. Bird's office.

I walked right up to Angela. "You! You were the one!"

"Mrs. Underwood, don't do anything you will regret!" Mrs. Bird warned me. She saw the anger in my eyes.

"Yes, don't." Angela said.

I didn't take my eyes off of Angela. I killed her with my eyes. "I won't. But you caused all of this mess! When you came to Atlanta I gave you a place to live! I fed you! I brought you here with me, helped you get your certification, and talked to Mrs. Bird for you! And this is how you repay me! Everyone will have their day! Even you, missy!" I said.

"Looks like you're having yours." Angela said.

"Mrs. Walker!" Mrs. Bird yelled at Angela.

"I am going to go to my class and teach my children." Angela said as she walked out of Mrs. Bird's office.

Mrs. Bird walked around from her desk and closed her office door after Angela walked out. "Mrs. Underwood, you cannot burst in my office like some maniac!"

"You said you were going to protect me! I don't feel protected! Looks like you forgot about me!"

"I am trying! The press was here this morning before I got here. They bombarded me probably the same way they did you! I was talking to Mrs. Walker about it before you came into my office." Mrs. Bird explained.

"What do we do now?"

"I don't know what we should do now! I have been inundated with parents calling me. And I haven't been here that long this morning. I told Mrs. Wells after so many to hold them all."

"Maybe I need to talk to my lawyer now." I wanted Mrs. Bird to reassure me that I didn't have to call my lawyer.

"Maybe. Just because I am not handling things the way you would handle them, doesn't mean I am not working. I am working." She was no longer confident.

"Maybe you should try doing more! More is always better."

"Don't tell me how to do my job. You are not in my shoes."

"And you're not in mine!" I stormed out of her office.

When I got home I told Mel about what happened. He cooked dinner as I sat on one of the barstools.

"It's going to be on television." I said.

"We are not going to watch it." Mel responded.

"It was probably on the noon news already. Everyone probably saw it. Everyone is going to know now. It is so embarrassing."

"How is it so embarrassing? We do not live for everyone. Who cares! You talked to your lawyer, right?"

"Yes. She went over some things with me, and she is prepared to do whatever she has to do. Baby, you are not ashamed of having a wife that is HIV positive all over television?"

"Did you really just ask me that? Baby, I don't do anything that I am going to be ashamed for. If I was going to be ashamed, I wouldn't have married you. I am a strong person, baby. You didn't marry some wimp. You married a man. A man doesn't need the validation of his peers or people he considers unimportant! You are important to me!"

"I envy you. You are so strong."

"I found some of your pills in the bathroom wastebasket. Do you know why?"

"I wasn't taking them, Mel. They were making me sick. I talked to my mother, and I am taking them now. Please don't lecture me. I don't need it right now."

"If you don't take your pills, you will not have to worry about fighting because you won't be around to do it. That is all I am saying."

"Babe, not now. Don't beat me when I am down."

"You not taking your pills is covert, Mrs. Underwood. No secrets in our home! I will not tell you anymore!"

"I am sorry."

"No need to be sorry. Just take your pills! It's you and me against the world. Not you against me."

"Oh, God! Mel they are just pills. I didn't cheat on you!"

"You might as well. You are killing yourself! These pills help keep your immune system strong!" He was furious.

"Babe, I am sorry. Please don't be mad with me. I will take the pills. They just don't feel like they are keeping me strong. They make me weak. But I bought a pill grinder the other day, so I will take my pills every day now. I promise. I really mean it this time! I want to live a long time to be with you, baby."

"I believe you. If you don't do right this time, I am going to start giving them to you myself. Now it's over, and it is time for us to have dinner. No more secrets."

"No more secrets. I promise."

"Well, you talked to your lawyer, so we wait this thing out while you continue to teach. You have four choices if worse comes to worse: fight to teach there, go to a public school and teach, stop teaching period because you don't have to work — you choose to, or start your own private school program."

I giggled at the thought of starting my own school. "Baby, I can't start my own school?"

"Why not? Someone had to start that school. You can do anything you put your mind and money to. Nothing is impossible. Nothing!"

"You're right."

"I know I am. Well, we have spent ten minutes on this, and that is all the time we are going to give it. We will not talk about this anymore. I don't want our house to become a place of war."

"You act like you're at least ten years my senior. You always have the right words to say."

"I say the right words because you are the right person, Mrs. Underwood." Mel kissed me.

The very next day, Mrs. Wells walked into my classroom and distracted me. Surely Mrs. Bird wanted to see me again.

"One minute class." I walked over to address Mrs. Wells.

"Mrs. Bird wants you to send Barbie Calls and Lowess Lane with me." Mrs. Wells explained.

"Oh, okay." I was relieved. "No problem. Barbie and Lowess follow Mrs. Wells." I thought nothing of it because kids were called to the office all the time. Some were called for early dismissals, medication, and to do announcements.

The students walked over to Mrs. Wells. "Please get your things children." Mrs. Wells told the students.

When she told them to get their things I was a little perplexed because the day had just started. I walked back over to Mrs. Wells. "Why do they need their things, class just started?"

"Mrs. Underwood, you will have to ask Mrs. Bird. I am just the messenger bringing the message. Come on, kids." She said.

I walked out into the hallway and stuck my head in Mrs. Dunns' room. "Mrs. Dunns, can you keep an eye on my class for me?"

"Sure." Mrs. Dunns said.

I walked swiftly to the office — not far behind Mrs. Wells and my students.

Mrs. Wells handed the kids to another first grade teacher that was in the office.

Mrs. Bird saw me come into the office. "Mrs. Underwood, go into my office! I will see you in there." She took control of the situation before I could say a word.

I sullenly went into her office and awaited her to accompany me. I was so angry that it felt as if Mrs. Bird took her time coming into the office. It wasn't that long. I prayed for God to calm me down. I didn't want to make things uglier than they already were.

She walked in the office all slow with those heavy conservative hips of hers. She had hips that I hated to see in a skirt. When things were out of control she always responded as if nothing was wrong. I guess that's why she was a great principal. She never panicked about much at all.

"Mrs. Underwood, I know you are upset." Mrs. Bird said as her heavy conservative hips slowly found a seat behind her desk. If the building was on fire, I don't think she would move any faster. I guess it takes time to move hips that heavy. Normally her hips wouldn't disgust me so much. But the fact that she could be so calm at a time like this, made me pick her apart in my head.

"Where are my students—"

Mrs. Bird interrupted me. "You saw them. They are going to be moved to another class just for now."

"Just for now! Why? I am a great teacher!"

"The parents are—"

I interrupted her. "Since when do we do what parents want around here? You run this school, Rolena! Parents have their children here because we produce! You don't want to fight!" I tried to make her remember I knew her before she became Principal Bird. I knew her when she had lent on her cheap skirt suits because she couldn't afford to put them in the cleaners. I knew her when she was crooked-teeth-Rolena. Now she has a raise in position and pay, has a fabulous weave, wears expensive suits that she takes to the cleaners, and beautiful veneers. She eats steaks and lamb for lunch. I remember when she sent to the burger joint like everyone else. She couldn't afford cheese on her burger. Ol' heifer! She upgraded, but I remember when, and I was going to make her remember too.

"It's not about fighting. It's convoluted —"

I interrupted her. "Rolena, are you serious! I mean are you really serious? Do you remember me when you were trying to be who you are today! Don't you play me! Why are those students being taken out of my class?"

"Listen, Mrs. Underwood. I worked my damn ass off to get this position, and I have worked my ass off to keep it! Yes, you were there for me, but I was here for myself! Now the parents of those children complained, and they wanted their kids taken out of your class!" She said. Those hips changed their tone fast. I was shocked to hear her curse. She was always calm and cool. I must have gotten under that weave.

"And you just did what they said? If they said they wanted you out as principal would you leave, Rolena?"

"No!"

"Exactly! But you want me to stay calm as you take my children out of my class. I am a damn good teacher that you should fight for! If it was your job on the line you would fight for it!"

"I am fighting for you!" It was silent. "I am trying to do my best here, but I am not a magician." She said calmly. "I have to satisfy the parents who pay their kids' tuitions. It's unfortunate, but that is the way things go around here. I am lucky that they didn't ask for the kids to be withdrawn. You still have your job. And as long as I have my job, you are going to have your job."

"What do I do?"

"I have to meet with the board members again — figure out this thing. I must placate the parents of the students right now."

"And while you are appeasing them, you don't stand by your teachers that help this school run? I understand exactly." I stormed out of her office.

Before I went back to my class I stopped in the restroom to clean my face. I had been crying. I said a little prayer, and asked God to forgive me for my evil thoughts about Rolena's hips. I was a changed person, and I was acting like the old Demisha. The old Demisha died when I vowed to

live my life for God. I had to remind myself of
that.

I went back into my classroom and taught my
class like the professional I was. Later on that day,
Mrs. Bird moved two more of my students into
another classroom. It hurt my heart, but I couldn't
do anything but watch it happen. Two by two
they went.

CHAPTER TWELVE

THE BATTLE IS NOT YOURS; IT'S THE LORD'S

When I arrived home Mel wasn't there. I took a bottle of wine, and I sat on the couch and cried my eyes out.

Mel walked in the house a few hours later. "Hey baby, why are you sitting in the dark?"

"I had a bad day." I answered.

Mel cut on the lights. "What happened?"

"Baby, today she took four kids out of my class. First she took two and later on she took two more."

"Why?"

I was somewhat intoxicated. "The parents complained. They wanted their children moved to another class. I guess I am such a threat to their children that they didn't want them around me. I take care of some of those kids better than their parents take care of them."

Mel flopped down next to me. "Baby, you are drunk. How much have you drank?" He took my glass out of my hand, and he looked around for the bottle.

"Yes, I have been drinking. I am tired, Mel. I met the greatest man in my life, and I can't enjoy him the way I should because my entire world is falling apart. I'm starting to think God doesn't love me. That has to be the reason." I cried.

"God loves you. You shouldn't say that! Your life is not falling apart. I better get you to bed." Mel stood up from the sofa and picked me up.

"I don't want to go to bed. I want to be with you." I slurred.

"I am going to take a shower, and then I will be right beside you."

"Baby, I am so tired. I don't think I can take anymore of this."

"Yes, you can. You are tougher than leather."

The next morning was Saturday. Mel was already up messing with pots and pans in the kitchen. I struggled to get out of bed. I felt a little dizzy. I held on to the handrail as I walked down the stairs. My equilibrium was off.

"Oh my God, my head hurts. What happened?" I said as I entered the kitchen where Mel was making breakfast.

"You drank an entire bottle of wine. That's what happened." Mel didn't look at me.

"Baby, I am so sorry. I came in yesterday, and I was very upset. Mrs. Bird removed four students from my class. She moved two that morning and two a little later. She wants to appease the parents in order to keep negative attention away from the school."

"So what are you going to do? Are you going to fight, go to another school, or what? You need to be ready to make a decision if you have to." He paused. "If these people are going to shone you, I say leave the school."

"I don't want to leave."

"Well, fight! But you can't come home every time something bothers you drinking whole bottles of wine. You are taking your medicine, and too much wine is not good with your medicine. Sit down and have some breakfast."

"Oh, baby, I don't feel like eating."

"That's why you need to eat." Mel placed a plate in front of me. "Now the way I see it, the reason she is doing what the parents want her to do is because she is in fear of the publicity the school will receive. I know that you don't want publicity either, but to get what you want you may have to go public."

"It's already public."

"Yes, but you may have to let the cameras into your life and into the school to show them that you are a loving teacher like all the other teachers. Well, like some of the other teachers. All teachers are not like you. See, if you do what she is afraid for the parents to do, she will try to appease you. The tables will turn." Mel sat down at the table with his plate.

"I don't know if I can do that."

"Baby, listen, I know this is serious, but even when things are serious I do not allow them to confuse me or make me stagnate. You have to do something. I take care of all the business decisions with the businesses. In business, the smartest person is the person that forces everything to be in their favor. I make moves that force everyone else to follow me."

"Baby, I am not like you. I just don't want to fight anymore. How many times do I have to tell you that?"

"Well, this is something that I cannot do for you. You have to do this yourself. But if you keep bringing it to me I am only going to tell you the same thing."

"The food is delicious, baby. But I cannot eat it all." I tried to change the subject.

"Thank you. Eat what you can." He put some food in his mouth and chewed it. "I am taking you over your mother's today."

"Why?"

"Remember you told her you were going to help her with the invitations and announcements for the pastor's anniversary celebration?"

"Oh, I forgot all about that."

"I know you did."

"Why are you trying to get rid of me? You're not cheating on me are you?" I asked humorously.

"Okay, you're not drunk now, so what's your excuse for being stupid?"

"Babe, why do I have to be stupid?"

"You asked me was I cheating on you. That's stupid."

"I know. I was just joking."

"I know. I was too. Eat up, so you can get to your mother's. If you remember you told her you would be there early. Mother is always on time with everything she does." Mel was frustrated with me.

"Yes, she is. I have had enough to eat. I am going to get a shower, so I can get over there." I didn't like Mel's energy.

After I showered and put my clothes on Mel dropped me over to my mother's house. He didn't talk much as he drove. My complacency annoyed Mel at times because he didn't understand it. Mel was a go-getter. He always had a plan. He was a fighter, and he didn't understand people who didn't fight for what they wanted.

****

Mother and I sat at her kitchen table. "What's going on with ya? Ya haven't said more than four words since ya been here." Mother observed.

"Mother, life is a mess right now. Everything is falling apart." I said fighting to hold back my tears.

"Child, what is falling apart? Ya have God, a

beautiful husband, a beautiful home, and ya health and strength. Life is pretty good from where I am standing."

"Mother, I have HIV, and I'm losing my job slowly."

"What happened?"

"You didn't see me on the news?"

"News! No, child! What is going on?"

"I am fighting for my job. Mrs. Bird took four of my kids out of my room Friday. The parents complained about me being around their children. I love those children."

"Ya don't have to convince me, child. I know. Why were ya on the news?"

"One of the teachers called the news on me. They wanted an interview. I didn't give them one. It's getting really bad, mother. I didn't tell you earlier because I didn't want you to worry."

"Listen baby, ya been through so much in such a short amount of time. But God is still smiling on ya."

"I don't see his smile."

"I do. Everything ya been through could have killed ya. But it didn't. He wakes ya up every morning. Ya still beautiful. Ya still have me. A lot of people don't have their mothers. Ya have Mel, a man that really loves you for better or worst. He has proved it! Some people take those vows and when the first problem comes they go runnin'. Not Mel—he has been right there with ya. Baby, ya sooooo blessed. See the good, and allow it to get ya through the bad."

I could no longer fight the tears. "Mama, I don't want to fight anymore. I am so tired. I am so drained. I feel like I am not going to make it." I sniffed. "Mel is getting tired of me. He wants me to be strong, and I'm not strong."

"Are ya kidding me? Ya my daughter! Ya gonna make it! Ya don't have to fight. The battle is not yours, it's the Lord's. And no one can beat the Lord! All ya have to do is be strong and stand. And when ya cannot stand, God will carry ya! How do ya think I am still here? My husband, your father, died shortly after we got married. I had to raise ya on my own. I had to put myself through nursing school to make sure I gave ya a better life. I had to put ya through college. I lost my father. But God! God brought me through it all, and I am not finished yet. I am now a minister—something I had no idea I would be. I am planning events now, something I didn't know I could do. I thought I was old, and God was finished. But he is not. Ya pray and do ya best. God will do the rest!"

"Mother, you always know the right things to say." I hugged her. Instantly her words restored me.

Mother and I had packed and sealed over 200

invitations and announcements. Then she and I spent the rest of the day shopping with Aunt Leana. I didn't make it home until later that evening. Mel walked out to Aunt Leana's car to help me with my bags.

"I see someone has been shopping. I was going to come and get you. Hey Aunt Leana. How is Uncle Bob?" Mel grabbed some bags from the car, and then he walked up to me and kissed me.

"He's okay, Mel. Probably waiting on me to get home and fix dinner." Aunt Leana said.

"Tell him I said hello." Mel said.

"I will." Aunt Leana replied.

"See you later, Aunt Leana." I waved to her. She backed out. "Mother, Aunt Leana, and I did a little shopping." I said to Mel.

"Did you get anything for me? I hope I got something in at least one of these bags." Mel said.

"I got you something." We walked into the house.

"You sound much better." Mel observed.

"Yes, mother and I talked. You know she just has a way of making me see the light."

"I know. That is why I reminded you about going. I knew you'd listened to her even if you didn't listen to me. She has a different method of saying what I say."

"Babe, you always help me too."

"I know, but it's just something about a mother and a daughter's relationship."

"You're right." I paused. "Oh, I am going to go before the school board and the parents to tell them my story."

"Baby, that's great! I told you, you are like me! It just took mother to bring it out of you. I am so proud of you right now!" Mel was ecstatic.

****

When I went back to school I had a positive attitude. My first stop was the front office. "Good morning, Mrs. Wells. How are you?" I said.

"I am well, and how are you?" Mrs. Wells responded.

"I am great. May I go in and see Mrs. Bird?"

"Sure. Just knock first. But she is alone."

"Thank you." I signed in and walked back to Mrs. Bird's office. Her door was cracked. But I still knocked on it before entering.

"Come in, please." Mrs. Bird said. I heard her moving around.

"Good morning, Mrs. Bird. How are you today?" I was purposely pleasant.

"I am well. I see you are doing great too."

"Yes, I am. Mrs. Bird, let me first apologize to you about the way I have responded to this whole situation. I decided that I would like to go before the board and the parents if I may. I would like them to hear my story from me."

Mrs. Bird looked startled. "I don't think that is a good idea. It will cause too much attention to the school. The parents may —"

I interrupted her, but I stayed calm and pleasant. "I understand the attention it will draw, but I need to speak out so that I can continue to teach my kids."

"If you do this, it is not certain that your children will come back to you. There is a great possibility that more parents will want their children removed from your class. What then? It will be out of my hands."

"That's the chance I am willing to take." I held my head high.

****

The day came for me to address the school board. The school auditorium was packed. There were parents from every grade level, all the teachers, the members on the board which included Mrs. Bird, news reporters that were invited by me, and my mother and Mel were there too. I stood onstage at a podium. I didn't write a speech. I just asked God to get rid of my nerves and fill my mouth with the words to say. He didn't get rid of the nervousness, but he did fill my mouth with words to say.

I took a deep breath. "Hi, my name is Demisha Underwood. I am a teacher here at Milton Academy. Many of you know me. God created me to teach your children. I have watched and assisted many of them in their growth as students and productive citizens of society. Today I am here because I am a teacher living with HIV." That's how I began my speech. The crowd was very attentive. In the beginning you could hear a pin drop. At different parts of my speech I was witty, and they laughed. The entire meeting lasted about two hours and thirty minutes. We had nurses there to educate the parents and the teachers about HIV.

When it was all over I stepped down from the stage and many of the parents and teachers walked by me and spoke encouraging words to me. I caught sight of Angela, and she didn't look very happy. She wanted things to get out of order. But it was civil and people really wanted to learn about the disease. Some of the parents shared with me that they had family members living with HIV. Therefore, some of them were already educated about HIV/AIDS. The news reporters interviewed me, and they were pleasant and on my side this time.

Mel and my mother walked over to me once I finished talking to the news reporters. "Baby, you did so well today. I told you! You were confident and secure up there. I am really proud of you!" Mel was exuberant. "You took control of the situation! You didn't let the situation take control of you!" Fighting for great causes excited Mel.

"Baby, ya looked beautiful onstage. It is going to be okay. I see God all over ya. God got this." Mother said. It was a bit noisy because people were exiting the auditorium.

"Thank you. I thought I was going to be afraid, but I wasn't afraid at all." I said.

"No, you were not. You were very confident, and once you finished you took a deep breath. I loved it! Epic!" Mel was hyped. I thought I was going to have to ask one of the nurses to give him a shot to calm him down.

"Ya spoke from ya heart. And people hear the heart more than they do anything else." Mother added.

"Wow. Thank you. Well, let's get out of here." I said.

"I think we should celebrate! Let me take my ladies to a nice restaurant to eat. No one has to cook tonight! My baby did what she had to do! She did her thang!" Mel said.

"Amen to that." Mother sounded.

****

After Spring Break, Mrs. Bird called me to her office. I had no idea whether it would be good or bad, but I decided to trust God. When I walked into the office I saw my students that were removed from my class.

"Mrs. Underwood, your students are ready for you." Mrs. Bird said.

"What! Mrs. Bird, thank you so much." I was pleasantly surprised.

"It wasn't me. It was you. I admire you. You're quite a woman, Mrs. Underwood. You're quite a woman." Mrs. Bird smiled. I hugged her.

The school board and the parents decided that I was not a threat to anyone. Mrs. Bird fired Angela because Angela tried to cause more trouble after she found out the school board decided to keep me on as a teacher.

In December of that same year, Mrs. Bird promoted me as head educator of our school, which accompanied a raise in pay, many accolades, and more benefits. The battle was not mine, it was the Lord's.

"Life is too great to live like it is too short."